BOOK ONE

BLOOD & LACE

VAMPIRE HEART

Don't miss these Bantam Starfire Horror titles:

BOOK ONE

BLOOD & LACE

VAMPIRE HEART

JOSEPH LOCKE

BANTAM BOOKS
NEW YORK · TORONTO · LONDON · SYDNEY · AUCKLAND

RL5.5, age 012 and up

VAMPIRE HEART

A Bantam Book / August 1994

*The Starfire logo is a registered trademark of Bantam Books, a
division of Bantam Doubleday Dell Publishing Group, Inc.
Registered in U.S. Patent and Trademark Office and elsewhere.*

ISBN 0-553-56614-8

Published simultaneously in the United States and Canada

*Bantam Books are published by Bantam Books, a division of Bantam
Doubleday Dell Publishing Group, Inc. Its trademark, consisting of the
words "Bantam Books" and the portrayal of a rooster, is Registered in
U.S. Patent and Trademark Office and in other countries. Marca
Registrada. Bantam Books, 1540 Broadway, New York, New York
10036.*

PRINTED IN THE UNITED STATES OF AMERICA

OPM   0 9 8 7 6 5 4 3 2 1

This book is dedicated to
DAN CURTIS
who created a landmark daytime
television show that had me rushing home
from school everyday as if my life
depended upon it. That show still holds a
very special place in my heart.

Thank you, Mr. Curtis, for *Dark Shadows*.

ONE

The Flight Home

Sabrina hated flying.

She sat in one of the seats inside her father's private jet as it sliced through the air, her seat belt on, head tilted back, eyes half open. The magazines on board were too boring to read, the music too dull to listen to. And even if that weren't the case, it wouldn't matter.

Her parents were dead.

Both of them.

"Can I get you anything, Miss Van Fleet?"

Sabrina looked up at the flight attendant and tried to smile, but did not succeed.

"No," Sabrina said. "I'm fine."

The woman smiled pleasantly, then left her alone.

Sabrina listened to the constant hum of the engines and thought about her mom and dad.

They had always been good to her. Unlike so many of her friends, she had never hated her parents. They'd had their disagreements, their occasional shouting matches. She'd even been spanked a couple times when she was a kid. But they always had encouraged and supported her in all of her endeavors . . . even the ones of which they did not entirely approve.

Sabrina couldn't believe that she was returning home to no family. Sure, there was Uncle Viktor, and cousin Jeremy, but she barely knew them. They came to live with her family shortly before she left for boarding school, nearly eight years ago. And she certainly wouldn't call Uncle Viktor comforting; he was older, odd, and distant. Jeremy was much younger—closer to Sabrina's own age—and he had a gentleness about him. Yet, from what Sabrina could remember, he, too, was emotionally, and physically distant. Even when Sabrina came home to visit, neither Viktor nor Jeremy seemed to be around much.

She still had her friends. While she was at the Bristol-Kitner School, Sabrina had always missed her friends back in Storm Point, but she'd made a great effort to stay in touch with them by phone and by mail, and she always saw them whenever she returned home. Especially Eric.

She had made new friends as the years passed, however. When she entered high school, she became involved in a few social clubs and was even elected president of the Photographer's Society. She was quite popular and had been getting wonderful grades from her first year onward. Her visits to Storm Point began to dwindle as she grew closer to her friends at Bristol-Kitner, but she never missed any of her friends at home —or her parents—any less. She kept in close contact with them all. Her parents had come to see her for the past two Christmas breaks. She had not been to Storm Point in well over two years, and even that visit had been short. It had been so short, in fact, that she hadn't even been able to see Eric, who had been in the middle of a big family reunion. So she hadn't seen Eric in nearly four years.

Her whole life had changed drastically in one fell swoop. A car accident, that's what she'd been told over the telephone. They'd gone over a cliff with Karson at the wheel. They had been killed, but Karson had lived . . . although he was in a coma and in critical condition, so how *long* he lived remained to be seen. But at least he was still alive. She had grown up with Karson at the wheel. He was a kind and gentle man with a wide smile that framed crooked teeth and made his eyes twinkle. Maybe Karson would come out of the coma and recover, she hoped.

She took comfort in the fact that Eric would be waiting for the jet to land at her father's private airpark. They'd been friends back when most of her friends hated boys and most of his friends hated girls. They'd teased each other at first, poked fun, made smart cracks at each other. But something had clicked. Back then, they'd liked the same toys and watched the same cartoons. Now they enjoyed the same books, listened to the same music, and liked the same movies. A month had not passed since she'd gone to Bristol-Kitner that they did not exchange letters and phone calls; sometimes there were two or three letters in a month, sometimes accompanied by pictures, magazine articles or comics clipped from the paper.

And now he was waiting to drive her from the airpark . . . because Karson was in a coma.

Depression lowered over her like a black cloud fat with rain. But at least Eric was there.

Eric had always been there for her . . . and she prayed he always *would* be. . . .

TWO

Waiting

Eric Jenning stood behind the four-foot-tall cyclone fence, staring at the runway of the Van Fleet Airpark.

Dusk was approaching, but it had been a dark and murky late summer day anyway, so it was hard to tell. Clouds the color of factory smoke—although there were no factories nearby—loomed overhead and a faint mist passed through the air like a throng of ghosts. There always seemed to be low clouds and creeping mists in Storm Point, Maine, even in August. In fact, they were quite common year-round. Some people said that winter came early and left late in Storm Point, and others said it *never* left; they were both very close to the truth. Winter seemed to hover close by and move in on its every whim.

Eric looked on anxiously for Sabrina. It had been a long time; so long that he was afraid he wouldn't recognize her.

Eric was not exactly the kind of young man most people expected to fit in with the Van Fleet family. His dad, Larry Jenning, was a construction worker and his mother, Dina, was the manager of a consignment store that sold used clothing, jewelry, books, and just about everything else. They lived in a small house in a small neighborhood—Eric, his eleven-year-old brother Nick, and their parents. They were nothing like the Van Fleets. Not at all.

And yet, they had accepted him. Eric and Sabrina had become such good friends as children that even their difference in social status could not separate them.

Eric stood at the cyclone fence and watched as the familiar jet touched down beautifully on the runway. A few minutes after the landing, Sabrina walked down the steps from the open door of the jet and headed for the gate.

She looked beautiful. Her shiny, full, dark blond hair bounced around her shoulders as she jogged toward the gate. She wore a white baggy sweatshirt with Bart Simpson's face on the front and a pair of jeans.

She came through the gate, and they slammed together in an embrace. A thick warmth rose in Eric's chest.

"Eric!" Sabrina said, her face buried in his shoulder.

They stood that way for a long time, in each other's arms. Then Eric said very quietly, into her ear, "I'm sorry. I'm so very sorry, Sabrina."

"Yeah," she whispered. "Me, too." They pulled away, hands still joined between them. "You're a sight for sore eyes, Eric. You look great."

"Me? Look at what all these years in England has done for you! You're beautiful!"

Sabrina blushed as they walked toward Eric's car.

"England's nice and I've made lots of great friends there, but . . . it's just not the same without you. Even with all the letters and phone calls."

Eric did not reply as he started the car and drove from the parking lot and headed down the road.

Sabrina watched Eric as he drove. He was no longer the little boy with whom she'd grown up. He was now a handsome young man with thick, windblown, rust-brown hair, beautiful dark brown eyes, and a body that was lean and fit. Almost involuntarily, she reached over and placed a hand on his shoulder because something inside her just wanted to touch him.

She frowned suddenly and bowed her head just a bit. "I just don't think it's ever going to seem like home again," she choked out, and began sobbing.

Eric's right hand left the steering wheel and reached out.

Sabrina moved her hand from his shoulder and clasped his hand tightly. It made her feel a little bit better. . . .

THREE

In the Mansion

The Van Fleet family had *always* had money. It went so far back that Sabrina wasn't quite sure exactly where or when the fortune had first begun to accumulate. All she knew was that the family had started one of the earliest—and, before long, the biggest—shipping companies, and the ever-growing fortune had been handed down from generation to generation.

After the winding ride up the hill, Eric pulled up to the elaborate black wrought-iron gate and stopped between the small video cameras on either side. The cameras stared at them like blank, mechanical eyes. Beneath each one, was a small round speaker and a microphone.

Sabrina rolled her window down, hung her arm out the door and smiled up at the camera. "It's Sabrina. Open up."

The black gates swung open slowly before them, its hinges releasing a high, metallic sound.

Eric drove through the gates and started along the lengthy oak-lined drive that curved this way and that.

The house was not visible from the gate. They had to

drive for a while up another incline before they began to see the lights shining eerily through the tall pines.

Then, quite suddenly, there it was. It wasn't even a house, really, although that's how they usually referred to it. It was a mansion. It was a very old mansion—it had been in the Van Fleet family for about two hundred years—but a lot of work had been done on it from generation to generation, and although it still looked like a very old, three-story mansion with ivy crawling up some of the walls, it was still in very good shape.

"Nothing looks different," Sabrina whispered as she watched the mansion grow larger as they drew nearer. "But I know it is. Everything will always be different . . . from now on."

Eric reached over and squeezed Sabrina's hand, but said nothing. Beyond the mansion, an obsidian sky stretched across the ocean, a sky that seemed to reflect Sabrina's mood. He pulled the car to a stop in front of the mansion, directly in front of the long, smooth, marble staircase that led up to the ornate double doors. Flanking the foot of the stairs were two granite lions rearing up on their haunches, their manes flowing as if blown by a wind, their jaws open to reveal intricately detailed fangs. In the glow of the lights at the top of the stairs, the lions almost looked real, as if they were about to pounce.

As Sabrina and Eric started up the steps, the dark oak doors swept inward and a plump, gray-haired woman wearing an apron hurried out, clapping her hands together.

"Sabrina, my darling!" the woman cried, her voice thick with a German accent.

"Elsa!" Sabrina exclaimed as they embraced.

Eric stood aside, smiling as Elsa whispered condolences into Sabrina's ear.

Elsa was the chief housekeeper, and a moment later, she was followed by her husband, Hans, the chief butler, a slightly stooped man with a balding gray head. He wore dark pants and a maroon tie beneath a gray vest; he'd removed his suit coat. He took Sabrina's hand, lifted it graciously to his lips and kissed it gently.

Sabrina grinned. Hans always kissed her hand. He was such a gentleman, and so cute with his ruddy cheeks and his sparkling eyes surrounded by wrinkled flesh. They were perhaps the only part of Sabrina's childhood left.

Elsa hugged Eric, too, and Hans shook his hand vigorously with a pleasant smile. Elsa hurried them into the house.

Sabrina bowed her head as a cold emptiness filled her chest. Her reason for coming home had hit her again.

As if reading her mind, Elsa patted Sabrina's hand and said, "Unpleasant circumstances, yes. And I am so sorry because your parents were such good, kind people. But it is so good to see you again, Sabrina."

"Yes, it is." The deep, rich, male voice startled all three of them.

Eric looked past Sabrina as she and Elsa jerked around.

Viktor Van Fleet stood behind and to the right of Sabrina, wearing his black Inverness coat. He was a very tall man with black hair that was short and slicked back against his skull. His face was a bit craggy and very pale, with sunken cheeks beneath high cheekbones. His closed mouth was curled into a lopsided smile. Before him, his hands were joined on the silver, snake's-head handle of his shiny black walking stick. His left hand lifted from the stick and moved slowly to Sabrina's shoulder, where at first it patted her gently, then came to rest.

"It is wonderful to see you again, Sabrina," he said, barely moving his lips as he spoke. "You are as lovely as ever."

She gave him a halting smile and stammered, "Uh, thank you, Uncle Viktor."

He turned to Eric and nodded slightly. "And you, Eric. It has been too long. You are always welcome here, you know."

"Thank you," Eric muttered.

Turning his attention back to Sabrina, Viktor said, "I can't tell you how sorry I am, my dear. But I assure you I will be here for you should you need me in any capacity whatsoever. And you need worry about nothing. I will handle all the necessary arrangements. Once again . . . my deepest sympathies, Sabrina." He looked gravely into her eyes for what seemed a long, long moment, then pulled his hand away and said, "I must go now, I'm afraid. I have things to take care of right now. Perhaps I will see you later this evening." With a slight bow at the waist, he turned and left the dining room just as silently as he had entered it.

Elsa made them a quick dinner, which Sabrina picked

at. Though she felt like she hadn't eaten in days, she had no appetite.

"Is Jeremy here, Elsa?" Sabrina asked while she played with her food.

"Oh, yes, he is," she said, keeping that smile. "He has given Hans so much help—that boy can fix anything. Cars, plumbing, the wiring. He is very handy. I will be sure to tell him you have arrived."

Elsa rushed off and came back a few minutes later with a young man, maybe eighteen or nineteen, trim and fit, with thick hair the color of ripe wheat that fell to his shoulders. He did not look a bit different than he had the last time Sabrina had seen him, which had been . . . well, years. He was *exactly* the same.

He was smiling, but his eyes looked sad as he spread his arms wide and hugged Sabrina.

"I'm really sorry, Sabrina," he said quietly as he stepped back, arms on her shoulders.

"I know," she replied, nearly whispering. "I really don't think it's hit me yet. But it will."

Jeremy shook hands with Eric.

"I'm sorry to rush off. The groundskeeper's pickup truck broke down and I told him I'd take a look, see if I can fix it. I'll be back soon."

"I guess I should go, too," Eric said. "You should get some sleep after that long flight."

Sabrina looked deep into Eric's eyes. She could tell that he didn't want to go, and she'd give anything for him to stay. She had an overwhelming desire to spend the night with him—he would love and protect her. But

Sabrina also knew that it wasn't right for her to spend the night with him for the wrong reasons.

She stepped forward and held him for a long time. "Thanks for everything, Eric. See you tomorrow."

He kissed her on the cheek and turned to leave.

"Eric—" Sabrina started.

He turned around quickly. "Yes," he said softly.

"Nothing," Sabrina said awkwardly. "Just, good night."

After Eric left, Sabrina went straight upstairs to her room with a cup of hot herbal tea, turned on some music and slowly began to get ready for bed. After brushing her hair at her vanity for a while, she turned off the music and her bedside light and crawled into bed. She was physically exhausted from the trip and mentally exhausted from everything else, so she was certain she'd have no trouble dropping off to sleep. That, however, was not the case.

She lay in bed *feeling* tired, but staring at the ceiling, wide awake, for over two hours. She tried to clear her mind, get rid of all the thoughts that were shooting around; she figured if she could just stop thinking, stop *remembering*, sleep would come and she would feel better in the morning. Finally, she turned on some quiet music, closed her eyes and took a few slow, deep breaths, thinking it might help.

But with her eyes closed, she kept seeing her parents' faces flash on the backs of her closed eyelids. When those faces refused to go away, Sabrina opened her eyes wide before she started to cry.

More time passed, slowly and silently with more tears. Until suddenly she heard voices.

They sounded angry and sharp and they rose and fell in volume, but she could not understand what they were saying.

Sabrina sat up slowly, frowning, and reached up to turn off the boom box on her headboard. It helped a little, but the words being spoken were still too garbled. She got out of bed, went to her door and opened it a crack, making the voices much clearer. After making sure there was no one in the hallway outside, Sabrina stepped silently out of her room, then stood to listen, able to catch only fragments of the conversation.

". . . do not *care* if you agree with me or *not!*" Viktor barked.

Jeremy's voice was lower, as if he were afraid they would be heard, but it was no less intense. He spat something at Viktor, but was not allowed to finish.

". . . not have you speaking to me that way, boy . . . will do as I say and . . . keep your opinions to yourself or pay the *consequences.*"

This time, Jeremy's voice was much clearer: "I'm not afraid of you, Viktor. I have no reason to be."

Viktor was silent for a long moment, then he snarled something too low for Sabrina to understand. But his voice grew louder, and as it did, the words dissolved into a wet growl . . . not the growl of an angry man, but that of . . . a wild *animal.* Gooseflesh crawled over the back of Sabrina's neck, as if a cold draft had just washed over her, and she stiffened her back as the growl became louder and fuller, wetter and deeper, until Sabrina took in a deep breath to scream for help.

Then it stopped.

There was a moment of quick, rustling movement downstairs on the ground floor, nearly inaudible from outside Sabrina's bedroom on the third floor.

She held that breath, her mouth open, her heart pounding so hard she could hear it in her ears. Letting the breath out slowly, she hurried around the corner to the landing and looked over the railing. She could see nothing, of course, but she'd hoped to at least hear something.

She did not. There was only silence downstairs, the faintly lit silence that comes once everyone has gone to bed.

After waiting a moment to make sure the shouting was over, Sabrina went back to her room, locked the door and got into bed. She didn't bother turning her bedside lamp off. She knew she would be too busy wondering what all that shouting . . . and growling . . . had been about to go to sleep.

With the exception of a little dozing now and then, Sabrina remained awake all night. She never felt so alone.

FOUR

The Funeral

The funeral was elaborate and Eric attended it with Sabrina, sitting beside her in front with the rest of the family.

Uncle Viktor was conspicuous in his absence, and Jeremy did not attend, either. Their absences made Sabrina curious. There were, however, a number of other relatives there, none of whom Eric knew and many of whom Sabrina had seen only in pictures or had met briefly at large family get-togethers.

Sabrina cried quietly throughout the ceremony, clutching Eric's hand tightly and using her other hand to dab her eyes with a handkerchief. She heard nothing that was said from the pulpit. She could only stare at the two closed caskets—closed because of the condition in which her parents had died in the car accident—knowing that she would never see them again . . . that they were dead and gone . . . and she was now alone.

Eric listened to bits and pieces of the eulogy, but was more concerned with Sabrina's state of mind. It made him sick to see her in so much pain. He knew she was holding back because she was there among all those other people; he imagined that, when she was alone, she would cry herself into a state of exhaustion. He wanted to be with her when she did that crying. He wanted to comfort her. He turned slowly to look at her. Even in her grief, she was beautiful. He was quite surprised by the way he'd been seeing her lately—as a beautiful young woman rather than just a *buddy*—and by how protective he felt of her.

When the funeral was over, Sabrina realized she would be expected to accept the condolences of all the people there. But she did not want to. She didn't want to talk to anyone about her parents' death right now . . . unless it was Eric. She leaned over and put her lips to his ear.

"Let's get out of here," she whispered. "Right now. I want to go home."

They did. They got into Eric's car and drove back to Sabrina's house, where she went upstairs to change her clothes. In a few minutes, Sabrina came down and met Eric at the bottom of the stairs.

Eric tossed a glance at the basement door and laughed. "Those locks are still there?" he asked.

"Yeah, they sure are."

"I remember when your dad put them there. He was afraid we might go down there and hurt ourselves."

"I remember, too," Sabrina said quietly, her voice unsteady.

Realizing he'd brought up painful memories, Eric put his arm around her shoulders and said, "I'm sorry. Let's go have a picnic, okay?"

Once they'd left the house, they walked silently for a

while along the edge of the cliff overlooking the ocean, Eric carrying the basket in one hand and holding Sabrina's hand with the other. He decided to keep quiet until she was ready to talk.

The sky was dark gray and fat with clouds that hardly moved, as if they were too heavy with unfallen rain to skid across the sky.

Sabrina was looking up at those clouds when she said, "Looks like we're going to get one of those nasty summer storms soon. I guess it's a good day for it. I mean . . . what's a funeral without dark skies and some rain, right?"

Sabrina's grip on Eric's hand tightened suddenly and she stumbled to a halt, startling him to a jerking stop as well. When he saw her staring with wide eyes and an open mouth at something before them, he followed her gaze slowly until he saw it.

The body of a large squirrel lay in the weeds a few feet before them. It lay on its side, still and dead, its small eyes collapsed in their sockets.

"It's just a squirrel," Eric said, stepping forward to stand over it.

"Yeah, but . . . *look* at it," Sabrina said, wincing. "It looks so . . . flat. Like a deflated balloon, or something." She paused. "That's enough to ruin lunch."

Eric took her hand again and they continued walking. "Well, let's just forget it, okay?"

They reached the path that wound steeply down the cliff and followed it carefully to the beach below.

Once they were walking barefoot on the moist sand of the beach, Sabrina set the picnic basket down. There were small rocks all around them holding tide pools filled with brightly colored starfish and sea anemones.

"You seem to be holding up pretty well," Eric said cautiously as they headed for the tide pools. "You sure you're okay?"

She took his hand and said, "I'm numb. I'm not . . . *anything* right now. I'm glad the funeral's over. I couldn't get out of there fast enough. But I don't want to be in the house, either. Too many memories, you know? Too many . . . ghosts. I just wanted to get out . . . come down here . . . be with you, and—"

She suddenly froze in place, rigid as a board. Then she began to sob uncontrollably. Eric went to her side immediately, put an arm around her and held her close.

"I-I'm suh-sorry," she sobbed.

"Don't apologize. You've got every reason to cry your head off, so just go ahead and do it."

After a few minutes of crying freely, she calmed down, backed away from him and wiped tears from her face with both hands. "I'm just so exhausted. I hardly got any sleep last night. I just want to . . ." She finished wiping the tears away, took in a deep breath and let it out slowly, then looked at Eric with wide, moist eyes and said, "Can we just forget about all this for a while? Pretend it didn't happen, maybe? I mean, just for now? Let's go catch some hermit crabs, or something. Like we did when we were kids, okay?"

Eric smiled. "Whatever you want."

They went to the tide pools and played with the scurrying hermit crabs, then climbed over large wet rocks and lay on their stomachs to look down at the clear water and the brightly colored creatures within it. All the while, their faces remained close together; sometimes their cheeks even touched as they looked down admiringly at the colorful starfish and sea anemones.

They turned to each other spontaneously and quite unexpectedly, their lips less than an inch apart. They kissed, slowly and gently. When they backed away, they looked at each other briefly, their eyes locked together.

Sabrina smiled slowly and said, "How about some lunch?"

Eric smiled back. "Sounds good."

They opened the picnic basket and spread the food out on a small blanket before them on the sand. There was cold chicken, potato salad, sour dough rolls, raw vegetables, fresh strawberries, and a Thermos of fruit juice. They ate in silence for some time, then Eric spoke up.

"Hey, your birthday's coming up pretty soon."

"That's right, it *is*, isn't it? With everything that's happened, I completely forgot about it."

"I think we should do something special, don't you? Just the two of us?"

Suddenly, their eyes locked and they stared at each other, still and silent. After a long moment, Sabrina whispered, "We kissed."

"Yeah. We did."

"So . . . what do you suppose that means?"

"Well, I think it means we've grown up and . . . we still feel the same about each other as we always did. Only, um . . . more, maybe."

A grin burst over her face. "Yeah, I guess so."

They kissed again, too, once the picnic basket was packed and they were ready to go back. It was a long, warm kiss, and when they finally pulled away from each other, they did so slowly, reluctantly, then returned hand in hand up the path, their bodies close and bumping each other as they walked. They were careful to avoid the dead and withered squirrel on their way back to the house. . . .

A Warning

E ric stayed with Sabrina until late and stopped at Taco Bell to get something to eat. He ordered a couple soft tacos and a burrito to go, then returned to his car, got in, slipped the key into the ignition and—

"Hello, Eric."

Eric let out a sheeplike bleat as he stiffened in the seat and turned to his right to see Sabrina's uncle Viktor sitting there.

The car had been locked. Eric *always* locked the car, it had become a habit.

The man sat in the passenger seat with his walking stick planted firmly on the floorboard, both hands folded over the handle and the cape of his Inverness coat gathered in great folds around his shoulders and arms. The lights of the restaurant were reflected sharply in Viktor's eyes, as if a tiny bit of shiny steel were imbedded in each retina.

"Yes, I know you are surprised, my boy," Viktor said with a smirk. "But don't be. I would like to have a word with you. Away from Sabrina."

"Yeah, well, I just . . . I-I-I'd kinda like to know how, um, how you . . . how you got into the—"

"Let's not waste time with such unimportant matters as that. I have some things to tell you, my boy. And I expect you to listen."

"Listen . . . to what?"

"To this. I would like you to stay away from my niece."

Eric blinked several times as he stared, his mouth still open. His lips and jaw worked a few times, but nothing came out for a long moment. "Stay away from Sabrina? Why? I mean . . . what are you talking about, *why?* We're best friends! I . . . I . . . I *love* Sabrina!" he barked, a bit surprised by his own words.

"Yes, yes, so I suspected. But you must understand one thing. Sabrina comes from a family that is very close, very much in touch with its roots. It is a family that has a long background of tradition to which it has remained very faithful over the years. Sabrina is a part of that tradition. You, however, are not. Therefore, I cannot stand by while you, however unintentionally, interfere with the ways of her family. Therefore, I am asking you to step aside quietly and willingly, as a gentleman."

Eric's mouth was suddenly dry, but he gulped before asking, "Step aside for what reason?"

"So that the family tradition may go on. I am certain you would not expect England's royal family to allow one of their young members to associate with a commoner. Do you understand? You were a friend of Sabrina's in childhood . . . but adulthood is quite different, my boy. It is over. Your relationship has come to an end."

Viktor opened the door on his side as he gave Eric a slight smile, the corners of his mouth curling up slowly like the tails of snakes. "It has been a pleasure, Eric. But I do not expect to see you again around the mansion . . . or around Sabrina. Keep that in mind."

He got out of the car and slammed the door.

Eric blinked a few times, recovering from the surprise, then looked out the window to see where Viktor was headed.

He was gone.

Eric looked in all directions, even out the back window, but the man was nowhere to be seen.

Eric sat there for a long time, stunned and confused . . . and most of all, hurt. . . .

SIX

A Late-Night Guest

Sabrina did not want to repeat the sleepless tossing and turning she'd gone through the night before. Tonight, she would rid her mind of all the worries and nagging questions that had come about in the last few days, and she would sleep.

Everyone else had gone to bed, even the staff. Sabrina went to the kitchen, made herself a large cup of hot cocoa and took it up to her room very carefully to avoid spilling any of it. She left her bedroom door open behind her as she crossed the room to place the cup on her bedside table, then kicked her shoes off her feet and reached down to pull off her socks. That was the only reason she heard the sounds downstairs.

She heard quiet voices, laughter, and a couple of clumsy and loud bumps against the furniture.

Sabrina froze in the middle of her room on the way to close the door.

"Not again," she whispered to herself as she stared at the open door, listening.

The voices continued, jovial, even giddy. One was low and deep, the other high and musical.

Just as she had the night before, Sabrina left her room and crept quietly into the hall where she turned left and headed toward the sounds that were coming from downstairs. As she leaned against the railing, the voices became clearer, but she could see nothing.

The deep voice was Uncle Viktor's; the other voice was that of . . . a *woman*? Yes, it *was* a woman, and she was giggling.

Sabrina started down the stairs very slowly and the voices became more distinct.

"No, no, my dear," Uncle Viktor said, "you do not want to go that way. Come with me."

"With you?" the woman replied, her speech slurred. "Ooooh, where we goin'?"

"You'll see, my dear, you'll see."

There was another thump, followed by the rattling of something made of thick glass, perhaps a vase.

When she reached the second-floor landing, Sabrina dropped to her hands and knees and crawled to the railing, trying to stay in the shadows and out of sight.

Below her, Sabrina saw Uncle Viktor coming from the enormous foyer; at his side was a young woman—maybe in her early twenties—wearing a long, ragged, brown coat and too much rain-smeared makeup, and with soaked blond hair that fell over her shoulders in long wet strands.

Something about what she saw made Sabrina feel very cold all of a sudden. Her flesh crawled and she felt her hands begin to tremble. But she did not make a sound as she watched Uncle Viktor lead the unsteady and obviously inebriated young woman past the stairs and down the hall toward the back of the house.

Once they were out of Sabrina's sight, she crawled to the stairs and hurried down silently, steadying herself with a tremulous hand on the banister. When she reached the bottom of the stairs she stopped, seated herself on the edge of a step and very cautiously peered around the corner to look down the hall. She saw their backs as they walked into the shadows of the unlit hall-way; the young woman leaned on Uncle Viktor, who put an arm around her waist and supported her as they began to blend into the shadows more and more.

Uncle Viktor has a date? she thought. *Why is he taking her down there? The only thing down that hall is the laundry room, some linen closets, a utility closet, the basement, and the way out to the patio! What is he doing?*

"Ooooh, it's gettin' dark. So, is your room down here, or what?" the young woman asked as she continued to lean against Viktor on the way down the hall.

"Well, I don't know that I would call it my room," Uncle Viktor said with the hint of a smirk in his voice, "but it is certainly where I spend a good deal of my time."

Sabrina felt her muscles tense involuntarily as they completely disappeared into the darkness.

Suddenly, she heard the sounds of locks being unlocked with solid clicks. There were no other sounds in the house, it was completely silent.

"Mighty safety conscious, aren't you?" the young woman asked.

Uncle Viktor replied, "One can never be too careful."

Their voices traveled like ghosts through the darkness at the far end of the hall. A door opened, then closed a moment later, and there were the muffled sounds of locks being turned on the other side.

Sabrina's face tightened into a frown as she stared into the darkness, wondering where they had gone. The basement, perhaps? It was the only locked door in that hallway.

She stood on the stairs and stepped down to the floor, rounded the corner slowly and cautiously, then started down the dark hallway. She moved slowly to give herself a chance to adjust to the darkness. In a few moments, she was able to see the doors of the linen closets, the utility closet, and the laundry room . . . and directly across from the laundry room was the door to the basement.

Sabrina went to the door, spread her arms and pressed a hand to each side of the doorjamb, then cocked her head to the left and turned her right ear to the door.

The voices continued, muffled now, as footsteps made their way loudly down the wooden staircase.

She wrapped her right hand around the doorknob slowly and tried, very carefully, to turn it. Locks on the outside were open, and the knob turned. But the door was locked on the inside, as if by one or more bolts.

The voices faded, along with the footsteps on the wooden stairs.

Sabrina did not move.

She heard the young woman's voice rise in volume; a sharp moan rose from the depths of the basement, again and again.

Sabrina rolled her eyes as she asked herself silently, *He had to go to the basement for that?*

Embarrassed, Sabrina turned away from the door, but something stopped her, made her freeze in her tracks.

That young woman's moan from down in the basement—the one that had seemed to be a sound of delight a moment earlier—suddenly sounded different. Suddenly—for just a moment, a cold and paralyzing moment—it became a sound of pain.

Sabrina's eyes widened and she listened very carefully for a moment, then turned back to the door.

By then, the woman was laughing and saying something that was muffled by the basement door.

Sabrina hurried away from the door and back up the stairs to her room. She undressed quickly, put on her nightshirt and got into bed after turning on some music.

She was just drifting off to sleep when she heard the faint sound of a distant scream. Her eyes snapped open and she stared at the ceiling as a chill passed over her.

The scream faded in such an echoing, dreamlike way that, a moment later, Sabrina wondered if she'd heard it at all. The sound did not come again. The house was, once again, completely silent. Only the hiss of the falling rain and the scratching of windblown tree branches against the windows of her bedroom disturbed the calm of the house.

It was the beginning of another night in which Sabrina got very, very little sleep. . . .

An Invisible
Wall

When Sabrina awoke the next day and rolled over in bed, she was shocked to see that her digital clock read 2:27 P.M. At first, she couldn't believe she'd slept that late . . . but then she realized that the last time she'd looked at that clock, it had read 5:34 A.M.

She shot out of bed and stood in the middle of her room, wiping the sleep from her eyes. She'd gone to sleep so late last night—or, rather, so early that morning—that she had every reason to sleep in till such a late hour, but it still bothered her; oversleeping always made her feel as if she might have missed something. Of course, these days . . . there wasn't much to miss.

She took a quick shower, dressed, then went downstairs. She met Elsa on the second-floor landing.

"Elsa, you should've woken me."

"No, no, dear. You need all the sleep you can get."

"Well . . . has Eric been here? Has he called?"

Elsa shook her head. "No, no one has come or called. I will be right down to fix you a nice brunch. I won't be a moment."

Sabrina went down the stairs with a frown on her face. She went to a phone and called Eric's house.

The line was busy.

She called again . . . and again and again . . . but the line was still busy.

Sabrina knew Eric's parents worked during the day, which meant that he and Nick would be the only ones left at home. But she also knew that Nick kept himself very busy with his friends and spent little time at home during the day. So chances were that Eric was the only one there. It didn't bother her that he was talking to someone else—Sabrina and Eric had a lot of friends in town, friends she was eager to see now that she was back —but she was a little surprised that he hadn't at least called by now. After all, it was late in the afternoon.

She tried his number a few more times and still got a busy signal. Then she decided to sit down to Elsa's brunch, even though she didn't feel all that hungry. . . .

Eric was alone in the house. His brother was spending the gray day with some friends playing baseball in the park. Sitting in his dad's recliner with a soda on the lamp table beside him, Eric stared at the television. The volume was up much louder than usual, blaring some afternoon cartoons that Eric was ignoring even though he was staring directly at the screen with a wrinkled brow.

He was chewing on his fingernails. It was a habit he'd had for years, much to the chagrin of his mother. He'd managed to overcome it these last two years or so . . .

but not now. His teeth were chewing at his nails just as voraciously as his guilt was chewing at his gut. And every now and then, he glanced across the living room at the telephone. The receiver was off the hook and stuffed beneath a pillow on the sofa so that the sofa appeared to be taking a call.

Eric, however, was *not* taking any calls . . . especially from Sabrina. Not for now, at least. He needed a little time to decide what to make of his encounter with Uncle Viktor the night before.

He hadn't slept well once he'd gotten home and gone to bed. He'd kept hearing Uncle Viktor's deep, level voice, so quiet but so crystal clear as he gave his little warning. It still seemed so bizarre that it would have been easy to think he'd dreamed it, but Uncle Viktor had been in his car all right . . . even though the doors had been locked. How had he gotten in? How had he known where to find Eric? And once he'd gotten out of the car, where had he gone so quickly?

Eric had been running those questions through his mind again and again as he stared at the television and glanced occasionally at the telephone.

How could he possibly do what Viktor had told him to do? He couldn't just walk away from Sabrina, especially now when she needed him so much . . . and now that their relationship had begun to change . . . to grow.

And yet, there had been something very ominous just beneath the surface of Viktor's words, even in his slight shadow of a smile.

The questions seemed endless, the answers invisible

and the time couldn't have passed more slowly had he been watching grass grow. But he had nothing else to do. Normally, he would be with Sabrina . . . but he couldn't go over there now, not after last night. Even if he tried, he wouldn't be able to hide his nervousness.

Of course, he could try being honest with Sabrina . . . but how? *Sabrina, your uncle Viktor told me to stay away from you because I'm not good enough for you . . . or I don't fit in with the family tradition . . . or something like that.* It sounded stupid. She would laugh, she'd think he was joking and she'd give him a little kiss for trying to cheer him up.

No, he'd just stay right where he was, in front of the television, watching *The Mighty Morphin Power Rangers* battle giant monsters . . . without really watching them at all.

That was when he heard a car pull up in the drive-way. . . .

Sabrina killed the engine and got out of the car. She couldn't tell if anyone was home or not, so she went to the door and punched the bell. She could hear the television playing inside, but there was no answer for several long seconds.

After waiting a while, she rang the bell again. Still, there was no answer.

"Eric?" she called. "Hello? Anybody home? Nick? Anybody?"

She tried the door, but it was locked. Just as she turned, frowning, to go back to the car, she heard the front door open with a soft, almost cautious click. Sabrina spun around to see the door open a few inches and Eric peering out at her sheepishly.

"Eric!" she said with genuine surprise. "Is everything all right? I've been trying to call you since about three and the line's been busy."

"Oh, well . . . maybe Nick left it off the hook accidentally, or . . . something."

She stepped closer to the door and—although she wasn't quite sure—thought she saw him move back just a bit. For a moment, his eyes left hers and looked beyond her, darting this way and that.

"Eric, what's the matter?"

"Um, I think I've got some kinda flu, or something. I'm not, uh, feeling well at all. Maybe you shouldn't get too close. You know, you might . . . catch it."

"You've got the flu in the summer?"

"I guess so. Do, um, viruses pay attention to that sort of thing?"

She laughed in spite of her concern, and it made her feel a little better. "I guess not. Look, Eric, I'm not worried about catching it. Are you alone? I can come in and take care of you till your parents get home, if you'd like."

"No, no, that's okay. I think I'm just gonna go back to sleep. I've been sleeping on the sofa all day."

"Oh. Okay. Well . . ."

"Um . . . how are you?"

"I'm okay, I guess. I was just looking forward to seeing you today. That's all."

"Yeah, me, too, but I don't think it'd be a good idea. I'm in pretty bad shape."

35

The door remained open only a few inches and she saw only part of his face.

"Okay. Well, at least put the phone back on the hook. And if you feel any better later, give me a call. Okay?"

"Sure."

They said goodbye and Sabrina went back to her car with a slowly tightening knot in the pit of her stomach. Somehow, she had a feeling that something was wrong, and it wasn't the flu. . . .

Even though Eric did not have the flu, he felt sick to his stomach by the time he returned to the recliner. He had wanted so much to open the door and embrace her. Under other circumstances, he knew they would've kissed, held each other for a while, then talked, maybe gone somewhere . . .

. . . but not today. Because today, Eric had a lump in his chest that he didn't quite understand and questions in his head that he could not answer.

He clenched both hands together under his chin as he frowned. He wasn't sick . . . but he really didn't feel well. And his state of mind was directly connected to his meeting with Viktor the night before.

Eric kept remembering Viktor's deep voice . . . the smug curl of his lips when he smiled slightly . . . and that silver glimmer in his eyes, like moonlight sparkling off the blade of a dagger. . . .

He hated to admit it to himself because he did not understand the reason for it . . . but deep down inside, Eric was inexplicably afraid. . . .

EIGHT

The Family Legacy

Sabrina had done nothing all day but putter around in her dad's library. The shelves of books reached to the ceiling and covered nearly every inch of the walls, except for the enormous leaded window at the back of the room, which overlooked the rose garden behind the house. She spent hours paging through the books that had been her favorites as a child, looking closely at the illustrations, remembering the voices of her parents, each of whom had spent a good deal of time reading them to her. She even shed a few tears, surprised when they fell with a *splat* onto the pages.

"Dinner is ready, Sabrina," Elsa said, stepping into the library with hands locked behind her back.

"I'm not really hungry," Sabrina replied without looking up from the book open in her hands before her.

"You are hungry, you just do not *know* it because you are wrapped up in all your *thoughts*! It is time to eat, so you come with me, my dear. Dinner is ready."

With some coaxing, Sabrina finally went with Elsa into the dining room, where Elsa pulled out the chair at the far end of the long table and pushed it back in beneath Sabrina as she seated herself. Once the food was served Sabrina ate without enthusiasm in the silence of the dining room, cutting at the chicken breast, poking at the vegetables and potatoes with her fork. When she felt she was being watched, she looked over her shoulder to see Elsa in the doorway of the hall that led to the kitchen.

"You are troubled, Sabrina," Elsa said quietly.

"Well . . . just a little lonely, I guess. Eric has, um, the flu. He says. And I just . . . I guess I'm not that hungry, is all."

Elsa smiled. "Would you like a little music? Some nice, soft dinner music? Good for the digestion!"

Sabrina managed a halfhearted smile and nodded.

Elsa disappeared through the doorway and a moment later, soft, soothing music came from the speakers hidden in the walls and ceiling of the dining room.

Sabrina bowed her head over her plate and took her food a tiny bite at a time.

"Sabrina, my dear."

The voice was sudden and seemed to come from nowhere. Sabrina jerked her head up to see Uncle Viktor sitting to her left at the table, his hands folded before him as his closed lips curled into a smile.

"Uncle Viktor," she blurted, her eyes wider than usual.

"Sorry if I startled you, dear. I thought I would join you for dinner tonight. If you don't mind, of course."

"Uh, no, no, that's fine, um . . ."

Elsa bustled into the room again and was about to say

something, her mouth open and ready to speak, when she noticed Uncle Viktor. She froze, staring at him. Uncle Viktor turned to her and said quietly, "Another serving, please. And I would like a glass of red wine, as well."

Elsa stared at him for another moment, then turned and disappeared. She came back a few moments later with Uncle Viktor's plate and his glass of wine. As Elsa hurried out of the room, Uncle Viktor touched the rim of the wineglass to his lips and tipped it a bit, never taking his eyes from Sabrina.

"Your birthday is coming soon," he said as he set the wineglass on the table softly, one side of his mouth curling up into a smile.

Sabrina looked at him for a moment, but did not respond; she simply went back to her meal.

Uncle Viktor began slicing his chicken breast lustily until the blade scraped the plate. Then he said, "You will be seventeen, correct?"

Chewing a bite of food, Sabrina looked at him and nodded, then swallowed and said, "Yes, that's right. Seventeen." She tried to smile at him, but she failed because . . . something wasn't quite right. The bite of food she swallowed seemed to stop halfway down and just sit there.

"Seventeen," Uncle Viktor said, letting the word ooze from his mouth as he sliced off another piece of chicken breast. "My, my. I remember when you were just a tiny baby. But now you are all grown up . . . and it is time for you to receive what is rightfully yours."

Sabrina was about to lift a bite of potatoes to her mouth, but froze. "What do you mean?" she asked.

"The family legacy, Sabrina. That is what I mean. Your parents—may they rest in peace—are gone, and now you are the next in line."

"The next in line for . . . what?"

"The family legacy."

"Which is . . . what?"

He tilted his head back and chuckled, never taking his eyes from hers. "Your birthday is coming, Sabrina. If I were to tell you now, there would be no surprise . . . would there, my dear?"

She frowned, but only for a moment. Then she shook her head slowly and said, "No, I guess not."

They chatted over dinner. Even though she had little appetite, Sabrina kept eating and chewing her food for as long as she could; that way, she wouldn't have to talk to Uncle Viktor much and he could just keep yammering on and on and on.

By the time Sabrina was done with her meal, Uncle Viktor was standing behind his chair and holding the black, silver-handled walking stick that had been leaning against the table the whole time.

"I must be going, Sabrina," he said. "But I want you to know I have enjoyed our time together. And remember . . . your birthday is going to be more important than you might think."

He bowed his head toward her in a gentlemanly way, then turned and left the room.

Sabrina leaned back in her chair and sighed. Then,

quite unintentionally, her eyes fell on Uncle Viktor's plate.

The food had been cut up and moved around . . . but he hadn't eaten a bite.

She looked at his wineglass and saw that, although he'd appeared to have taken a number of sips from it, the glass was just as full as it had been when Elsa had set it before him.

Sabrina stared at Uncle Viktor's plate for a long time, her brow cut with deep wrinkles as she frowned, and she whispered to herself, "Family legacy . . . legacy . . . what legacy?"

She got up suddenly, hurried to a phone and called Eric's number. Mrs. Jenning answered.

"Hi, this is Sabrina. Is Eric there?"

"Oh, hi, Sabrina," Mrs. Jenning said. "How are you?"

"Well, I'm doing okay, I guess. But how is Eric? When I saw him today, he was really sick. Is he any better?"

"Sick? Eric? When?"

"Well, I dropped by the house today. He said he had the flu."

There was a long silence, then: "Well, Sabrina, I don't know if he's got the flu or not because he seemed just fine when I got home this evening, but . . . well, he's in bed right now. He went to bed about twenty minutes ago. Maybe he's not asleep. I can get him if you'd like."

Sabrina's grip tightened on the receiver and she

frowned once again, pressing her lips together hard for a long, silent moment.

"Uh, no, Mrs. Jenning, that's fine. Let him sleep. I'll see him tomorrow."

"You're sure?"

"Yes, I'm sure. Take care. 'Bye."

Sabrina hung up the phone and stared at it for a long time, realizing that she was no longer sure of anything anymore. . . .

Carcasses

After breakfast the next day, Sabrina tried again to contact Eric. She called him a number of times, and each time she heard only Mrs. Jenning's recorded voice on the answering machine, apologizing for not being there and asking her to please leave a message. The first three times she called, Sabrina asked Eric to please call her back because she needed to talk to him, it was important . . . and then she gave up and simply hit the OFF button on the cordless phone as soon as she heard the recorded message.

Her parents' will was to be read that night and Sabrina was nervous. She wasn't quite sure why, but she felt like she was about to take a big, important test at school for which she was not prepared. She wanted Eric to be with her, but she had a funny feeling he wouldn't be . . . and she couldn't figure out why. Something was wrong. He'd lied to her about having the flu. In fact, he'd peered out of that front door at her as if *she* had some sort of plague, as if he was afraid to get close to her. And he'd looked around a lot, too, as if he were expecting something to happen. His eyes had darted this way and that, looking over her shoulders as if he'd been afraid someone might sneak up on him.

Sabrina was worried about him . . . about *them*. She kept wondering if she'd done or said something to hurt him, to scare him off. By noon, she was tired of wondering and worrying, and she got a lunch together to take down to the beach. The ocean always made her feel better about everything—the sound and the smell of it—and she wanted to take her mind off her problems for a while. She decided that if she couldn't reach Eric when she got back, she would go over there and insist that he speak with her, providing he was home. But somehow she knew he was there, ignoring her calls, just as he had done the day before when the receiver had been off the hook.

With her picnic basket in hand, she crossed the massive backyard and headed toward the cliff's edge on her way to the trail that would lead her down to the beach.

The day was, as usual, rather gray, but there were large patches of blue sky among the clouds. Sabrina stopped and looked up at them and smiled, finding them refreshing. She took a deep breath of cold, damp sea air, then continued onward. A chilly breeze passed over her again and again, but she'd become accustomed to that years ago and paid it no attention.

Her sneakered feet kicked through the weeds as she neared the edge . . . until her foot struck something. She froze and looked down.

It was a rabbit, with gray fur and big ears and long hind legs . . . and it was dead. But it was more than dead. It looked exactly like the squirrel she and Eric had found on their way to the trail: deflated and empty, as if its insides had been sucked out of it.

Sabrina gasped and slapped a hand over her mouth as she stumbled backward and made her way, very carefully, around the rabbit's carcass. She even picked up her pace, wanting to put it behind her as quickly as possible. She had enough to worry about without looking at dead, shriveled animals.

She was about ten feet from the trail when she saw the small deer less than two feet in front of her . . . dead and flat, its eyes sunken so far into its sockets that the sockets looked dark and almost empty.

Sabrina froze, staring at the dead animal. In all her life there on the top of the hill above Storm Point, she had *never* seen a single dead animal . . . especially one that looked like *that*!

She walked around it and hurried down the winding path to the beach, where she dropped the picnic basket, kicked off her sneakers, rolled up her jeans and walked out into the surf a little ways, enjoying the feel of the cold water as it rushed back and forth over her bare feet.

After eating her lunch there on the beach, she put her sneakers back on and did something she loved more than anything—she crawled over the enormous jagged rocks along the beach. She paused now and then to look down at the tide pools and the colorful creatures living in them, but she kept moving until she was on the rocks at the very foot of the cliff. She'd climbed them many times before throughout her childhood. There was one rock in particular that jutted up above all the others, a rock she liked to climb so that she could sit at the top and look out over the ocean as it roiled and raged, as its waves crashed against all the other rocks and slammed against the cliff face.

Sabrina climbed with only a few slips of her feet on the wet rocks, slips from which she recovered quickly. She finally made it to the top of the rock and perched herself there like a bird so she could look out over the ocean. But among the smell of seawater and the plant life the waves washed in, Sabrina smelled something else . . . an odor so foul that when it hit her full force, she slapped a hand over her mouth and began to swallow again and again to keep herself from gagging and throwing up her lunch. And as she covered her mouth, she looked down.

Below her, at the foot of the enormous rock upon which she was sitting, was the body of another deer, this one a bit larger than the last. It looked just as emaciated as the other animal carcasses she'd seen. But it was bent over one of the rocks below, as if it had been thrown from the cliff above.

Very slowly, Sabrina turned away from the flattened deer carcass and looked upward to the cliff's edge overhead. It was so far above her that she had to tilt her head backward sharply. There was, of course, nothing above her but the edge of the cliff . . . but she wondered what kind of person would throw a deer over the side and onto the rocks below.

She was about to turn her head away when she spotted something she'd never noticed before. She did a double take and looked back up at the cliff face.

Several yards below the edge of the cliff there was a

gaping black hole, shaped somewhat like a pear. It was a cave, completely inaccessible to anyone other than a daredevil climber. But it was directly above her . . . and directly above the wasted body of the deer.

Sabrina began to climb down from the rock immediately and head back to her picnic basket. Once she was there, she swept up the basket and hurried back up the trail.

As soon as she got back to the house, Elsa met her at the door. She looked glum and sorrowful—like she had just been crying.

"What is it?" Sabrina asked. "There *can't* be more bad news."

"I'm afraid so, my darling," Elsa said quietly, her lips quivering. "You see, we just got a phone call from the hospital. Karson died."

Sabrina reached out and hugged Elsa. Little by little, everyone in her life was slipping away. She cried and sniffed and sobbed for a long time, then decided she wasn't going to let go of the one person she had left. . . .

Caught Off Guard

When Sabrina rang Eric's doorbell, there was no answer. She rang it several times and waited and waited, while somewhere nearby, someone mowed their lawn.

Finally, Sabrina turned to leave, but when she looked at the houses all around Eric's house, she saw that no one was mowing the lawn . . . and then she realized the sound was coming from *behind* Eric's house. She crossed the front yard, opened the gate at the side of the house and walked to the backyard, where she found Eric pushing a lawnmower over the grass, back and forth, completely oblivious to her, his head hanging low as if he were depressed.

"Eric!" she shouted, heading toward him. She waved her arms and called his name a few more times until he finally heard her above the rumbling motor and turned to her with an expression of surprise on his face. He turned off the mower and started toward Sabrina with his fingers slipped into the back pockets of his jeans.

"You're mowing the lawn?" Sabrina asked. "You *must*

be sick. In fact, you look horrible. Do you have a fever? Have you been vomiting? Maybe you should be in bed." Her voice was tinged with icy sarcasm as she stood before him with one hand propped on her hip.

Eric held up his hands, palms out, and said, "Okay, okay. I'm sorry."

"For what? What's going on, Eric? And please, don't give me any crap. Have I done something?"

"No, you haven't. It's not you, it's just that . . . well, I guess it's me, that's all. Maybe I'm just scared to get so close with someone. . . ."

"Then we're gonna have to talk. I don't know what's wrong, but whatever it is, I want us to take care of it. I need you now, Eric, I really do. Karson died this morning."

"I'm so sorry," Eric said, embracing her. "I feel like such a jerk!" He kissed her. "I've missed you, Sabrina. I won't desert you again. I promise."

"Good," Sabrina said. "My parents' will is going to be read at the house tonight. I want you to be there with me."

"I want to be there for you if you need me. Is—is Viktor going to be there?"

"Probably. Why?"

He bowed his head a moment, shaking it back and forth slowly. "Nothing. I'll be there. Whenever you want. I'll go over there with you now, if you'd like."

"Would you?"

"Sure." He looked at her and gave her a gentle smile. "I just need to finish the lawn and then I'll change my clothes, okay?"

She nodded and Eric returned to the lawn-mower. . . .

As he changed his clothes in his bedroom, Eric frowned, worried and confused. What would Viktor do if he saw Eric there at the house with Sabrina? How serious was he about his warning?

Eric just hoped Viktor wouldn't show up. He was hardly ever around anyway, right? But Sabrina needed Eric, and he couldn't turn his back on her. He'd just have to stand up for himself!

But like Sabrina, Eric had always considered Viktor to be a little odd . . . but this was the first time he'd ever felt genuinely afraid of him. And Eric hated it. . . .

ELEVEN

The Reading
of the Will

By the time they arrived at the house, dinner was already under way and the dining-room table was surrounded by relatives, most of whom she hardly knew. She assumed they'd come for the reading of the will. She didn't feel up to dealing with *any* of them at the moment, especially when it came to the distribution of her parents' belongings.

Sabrina frowned as she stood with Eric in the dining-room doorway staring at the table. Uncle Viktor sat at the head of the table, leading the conversation, laughing his deep, rumbling laugh as he entertained all the others.

"I don't want to go in there," Sabrina whispered to Eric, and they backed away and disappeared around the corner.

In a moment, Elsa joined them. She looked disgruntled, aggravated, as if she'd rather be serving dinner to a grunting, broken-toothed group of hockey players.

"I do not know why they are here," she said quietly, pressing her hands together hard before her. "Apparently your uncle Viktor has invited them here, but I do not know *why*!"

"What about the will?" Sabrina asked.

"Oh, yes, Mr. Canby is in your father's study. He would like to see you as soon as possible. But in the meantime, I must serve these giggling dolts . . . and your cackling uncle. I do not like this at all, not at all. I have bad feelings. In fact, I do not even think I will be able to eat dinner myself . . . my stomach is in *such* a state."

Elsa waved a hand back and forth in front of her face, as if she'd been affronted by a bad smell, then turned and hurried away.

"C'mon," Sabrina said, taking Eric's hand, "let's go to the study. I'd like to talk to Lowell and see how soon we can get this over with."

They were there in about twenty seconds, and they found Lowell Canby—the Van Fleets' longtime attorney, a short, balding man with a fringe of curly silver hair around his head and the bushiest eyebrows Sabrina had ever seen—sitting behind Sabrina's father's desk with a briefcase open before him. He was frowning deeply as he shuffled through some papers, and he did not even hear them come in.

"Lowell?" Sabrina said.

When the older man saw her, he dropped the papers, shot to his feet and hurried around the desk toward them, embracing Sabrina for a moment, patting her back gently as he said, "Sabrina, sweetheart, I'm so very sorry about your parents."

"Thanks, Lowell," she said with a smile as she

pressed the side of her face against his shoulder. She'd known him for so long that he seemed more like a member of the family than the relatives having dinner in the dining room at the moment.

When they separated, Lowell turned to Eric. They had met only once, but it had been when Eric was very small, so he didn't remember the attorney. But Lowell remembered him and he moved forward and took Eric's hand, shaking it firmly as he grinned.

"Well, you've certainly grown into a fine young man, Eric, m'boy," he said with a chuckle. "Last time I saw you, I think you came almost to my waist, and you had trouble pronouncing my name. If I'm not mistaken, you kept calling me Mr. *Candy*!" He laughed loudly as he let go of Eric's hand.

Eric smiled and nodded. "Well, it's nice to see you again, Mr. Candy—I mean, *Canby*!"

Lowell laughed even harder.

"Listen, Lowell," Sabrina said, once his laughter had quieted, "how long before we can get on with this will-reading? 'Cause I'd really like to get it over with, if you know what I mean."

"Of course, Sabrina." He was solemn now, his laughter was gone, even from his twinkling eyes. "Well, now that you're here, we can do it whenever you'd like."

"But what about everyone else?" she asked.

"Who?"

"Those people in the dining room. All those relatives . . . and Uncle Viktor, and Jeremy!"

Lowell rolled his eyes as he turned and went back to the desk. Once he was behind it and seated, he gestured toward two leather-upholstered chairs positioned in front of the desk. "Please, sit down. Both of you."

After glancing at each other, Sabrina and Eric went to the chairs and seated themselves.

Lowell closed his briefcase, set it aside, put his elbows on the desktop and joined his hands beneath his chin. "From what I understand, those people were invited here by Viktor. I don't know where your cousin Jeremy is, but he's not involved either. You see, readings like this are by invitation only. Those who are mentioned in the will are the only ones invited. None of those people out there were invited. And that *includes* Viktor."

"Are you so sure about that?" a deep voice asked.

Lowell raised his head and Sabrina and Eric spun around to see Uncle Viktor standing in the open doorway, both hands clenched tightly around the walking stick's snake's head handle before him. His face looked hard as granite; his eyes were narrowed slightly and the thin lips of his closed mouth were curled downward beneath his hollow cheeks.

He remained there during what became a long and uncomfortable silence among them all. He did not move a muscle, did not even blink, just stared at them with eyes of cold steel and an expression carved out of icy rock.

Finally, Lowell stood. "Viktor, you know you were not invited to the reading of this will. Therefore, you have no reason to expect that you or any of the people out there in the dining room would be welcome. So why in the world would you invite them here with that in mind?"

"Because I know that I am in that will," Viktor said, moving only his lips while the rest of his body and face remained frozen. "I know that *I* am in that will, and the rest of those *people* are in that will. Donald and I worked on that will *together*, for *hours*, and I know it from *beginning* to *end*!"

"Well, I hate to disappoint you, Viktor," Lowell said with a trace of a sigh in his voice, "but Donald changed his will nearly a month ago. Therefore, it is no longer the will on which you worked with him. It is no longer the will you *know*. And you are no longer *in* it. Of course, if you'd like to know the exact date of alteration, I can look through the—"

"That is not true!" Viktor roared, pounding his walking stick onto the floor before he stalked into the room. "I am the chief beneficiary and have been for some *time*! Therefore, I *refuse* to listen to your talk about any alterations in the will, because I know *better*!" By the time he was finished stalking across the room, he was standing before the desk and leaning over it, pushing his angry face close to Lowell, who barely flinched as he tilted his head back and faced Viktor head on.

"I'm sorry, Viktor," Lowell said very quietly, but with controlled anger, "but I have only one will. I know what that will says, and what it says stands. If you have any complaints about that will, then I suggest you take your complaint to a court of law. Because in this room, your complaints hold no weight whatsoever."

"This is *ridiculous*!" Viktor shouted. *"I* am the chief

beneficiary of this will, and I will *not* accept this *lunatic* explanation of yours, Mr. Canby! If you have documents that give worth to another beneficiary, I would like to know who he *is*, and I would like to know *now*!"

With an expression on his face that resembled a sneer, Lowell placed both fisted hands on the desktop and rose from his chair, his eyes never leaving Viktor's.

"Listen to me very carefully, Viktor," Lowell said quietly, smirking. "The will that I have before me says that Sabrina is the sole beneficiary of the entire Van Fleet estate."

Sabrina gasped quietly at about the same time that Viktor released a strained grunting sound.

"Therefore," Lowell said, "you have nothing to do with this will . . . the reading of it . . . or the execution of it. If this displeases you, then I suggest you get a lawyer and deal with it in court. Otherwise, I suggest you leave this room, because you have nothing to do with the business that is about to take place here."

Very, very slowly, Viktor backed away. As he neared the doorway, his mouth twisted into a sneer and he made a sound that made Sabrina's back stiffen and her eyes widen.

It was a growl, more animal than human, and it came out of the side of his mouth as his lips parted on one side, ever so slightly. She remembered that sound. She remembered where she'd heard it before . . . and it frightened her.

"Good evening, Sabrina," he said. Then Viktor spun around and glared at Eric. "What a *surprise* seeing you, Mr. Jenning."

In an instant, Viktor disappeared, and they heard the front door slam heavily just moments later.

"I'm terribly sorry that happened, Sabrina," Lowell said quietly.

"Don't worry about it, Lowell. It wasn't your fault."

"Well . . ." Lowell shrugged and sighed. "I suppose that now anything I tell you will be redundant. You heard me tell Viktor. You really *are* the sole beneficiary. Because you are a minor, your aunt Caroline will be flying in this week from Wisconsin. She is now your legal guardian until you turn eighteen."

Sabrina blinked a few times, then the ends of her mouth curled up into a slight smile. She remembered Aunt Caroline very well from her visits to Storm Point during Sabrina's childhood. She was a chubby, red-cheeked woman with a ready smile and pleasant laugh. Sabrina remembered Aunt Caroline as one of the kindest of her relatives, a sweet woman who wanted only to please, who loved a good joke and who would rather die than do anything that might hurt someone.

"I look forward to seeing Aunt Caroline," Sabrina said with a smile.

"That's just what she said about you," Lowell replied with a satisfied grin.

Sabrina's smile dropped away as she glanced at the open doorway and asked, "Um, do you know where Uncle Viktor went?"

"No one knows where he goes," Elsa said as she scurried into the room with a tray of tea and cookies, complete with cups, spoons, sugar, and cream. "He just goes, every night. Then he reappears every evening."

She set the tray on a corner of the desk, then was gone as quickly as she had appeared.

"Oh, my!" Lowell gasped. "I forgot something." He returned to his open briefcase and removed a small, rectangular box wrapped in plain brown paper, then held it out in both hands toward Sabrina. "Your parents left this for you. The instructions are that you're to open it in private."

Sabrina looked at the box with wonder as she took it into her hand. "I will," she whispered. "Yes, yes . . . I will."

"Well," Lowell said with another smile, "what do you say we have some tea?"

TWELVE

A Gift
after Death

After chatting stiffly with Lowell over tea, Sabrina and Eric retreated to her bedroom, where she perched on the edge of her bed and he seated himself in a straight-back chair facing her.

"Are you sure you want to do this?" Eric asked. "He said you were supposed to open this in private, y'know."

Her face jerked up at him and her eyes widened slightly. "What are you talking about, Eric? This *is* private. He didn't say I had to be *alone*, right? And I *want* you here . . . because you're the only person I'd share this with."

For a moment, they looked into each other's eyes and a smile spread over Sabrina's face very slowly as she reached out for his hand. He took it and returned her smile as their hands squeezed each other.

"Really," she whispered, "you're the most important person in my life now. That's why I want to share this with you." Then, in a normal tone, she added, "So stop being so paranoid." She pulled her hand away and began to tear the brown wrapping from the box.

Beneath the paper was a white cardboard box with the removable lid fastened down with strips of tape on each side. She ran a thumbnail through the tape and removed the lid.

Inside, the box was filled with crumpled tissue paper, on top of which lay a narrowly folded piece of paper. Sabrina placed the box on the bed, removed the paper and unfolded it very slowly, as if she were afraid to read whatever might be written on it.

Her eyes scanned the page, then she took in a deep breath before reading it aloud to Eric.

Dearest Sabrina,

This is a final gift from us to you. Please wear it always. Perhaps it will make it easier for you to remember us in the years to come. In any case, it will protect you from the evil around you.

Please remember that everything is not as it seems. Do not assume, although you are home, that all those around you are loved ones. Instead, find the treasure within the house, which is now yours, before it can be taken from you. And please remember that closest to that treasure are your parents—and we have always loved you with all our hearts, ever since your first sharp cry.

Have a wonderful life, and always remember that you were the best daughter any parents could ever hope to have.

With all our love,

She held up the letter so that Eric could see their signatures. He leaned forward and squinted ever so slightly.

"That's their writing," she said quietly.

Then Sabrina put the letter aside and began to fish through the tissue paper until she pulled out a silver chain. Attached to the bottom of it was a small silver cross studded with tiny diamonds. The diamonds were channel-set in the silver, three horizontally, four vertically.

"My God, it's beautiful," Sabrina whispered in awe as she lifted the cross before her. "Would you *look* at this? It's absolutely *gorgeous!*"

Eric left his chair and seated himself beside Sabrina on the edge of the bed so he could see the cross.

The diamonds sparkled in the light as the cross turned this way and that on the chain.

"It's beautiful," Eric said quietly.

"But why?" Sabrina asked in little more than a breath.

"Why? What do you mean?"

"Why did they give it to me?"

"Well, obviously because they wanted to leave something for you to remember them by."

Her hand dropped suddenly, plopping the chain between her thighs. "But how did they know they'd go *together*? They *both* signed this letter! And why did they write, 'it will protect you from the evil around you'? Huh? What about 'do not assume that all those around you are loved ones'? Why did they write *that*? What does that *mean*?"

Eric's back stiffened and his eyes widened a bit as he shrugged. "I don't know, Sabrina. Really. Why do you think it's important? I mean, after all, the cross is a religious symbol, so—"

"No, no, no. My parents were not that religious. It's not something they would write to me. They weren't like that, really. I mean, the word 'evil' is something they'd never even use in conversation. *Ever!*"

Eric started to get worried and tried hard not to frown as he looked at her. "So . . . what're you saying? That they didn't write the letter?"

"Of *course* they wrote the letter! This is their handwriting! They *both* signed it!"

"Okay, then. So what is it that's, um . . . what's bothering you?"

She lifted the chain from her lap with one hand and lifted the letter with the other, looking from one to the other, back and forth.

"What bothers me is that the letter they wrote to me sounds like . . . well, y'know, like a *warning!*"

"A warning?" Eric asked, flinching slightly. "A warning about *what?*"

"I'm not exactly sure, but . . . well, I think it might have something to do with Uncle Viktor."

As she paced back and forth, she told him what she'd seen two nights before, late at night . . . Uncle Viktor and his drunken female guest . . . and the fact that they had gone into the basement.

"It was locked from the *inside, too,*" she said as she stopped before him, her words heavy with significance.

"Well, your dad had the basement locked up a long

time ago. In fact, I remember when he did it. We were just little kids and he was afraid that—"

"From the *inside*? Why would he do *that*? In fact, *how* would he do that?"

Eric was getting more and more nervous, and he wasn't quite sure why. He was all too certain, however, that the reason would come to him soon.

"I heard a scream," she continued.

"A what?"

"A scream. That night. I came back up to my room, ready to ignore the whole thing . . . and I heard a scream. It was a long, muffled . . . horrible scream, Eric. Horrible. At first, I thought I was dreaming. I guess I was *hoping* I was dreaming. But I wasn't. That woman he took down to the basement . . . she screamed. He *did* something to her."

"Did you, stick around to see if she came back out?"

"I stayed awake, I can tell you *that*. There were no more voices downstairs. Nothing. Just silence. In the whole house. Eric, I . . . I don't think she ever came back out of that basement."

Suddenly, Eric could no longer remain in the chair. He stood and began to pace back and forth as well.

"Sabrina, I'm not sure what you're telling me. That he *killed* this woman? That he . . . I don't know, that he . . . *what*? Please, *tell* me!" he said as he stopped, standing inches in front of her, looking into her eyes . . . her beautiful, deep brown eyes.

"Think about it," she whispered. "Mom and Dad left me a *cross* . . . to protect me from the evil that they think surrounds me. They tell me that not everyone

63

around me is a 'loved one'. They say there's a 'treasure' in the house that I should find before someone else takes it away from me. There were warnings, nothing but *warnings* in that letter."

THIRTEEN

Jeremy's Story

They moved to the breakfast nook, where they made some coffee.

"Okay, let me make sure I understand this," Eric said quietly, his head cradled in both hands while his elbows rested on the tabletop. "You want us to get into the basement while Viktor's out . . . but it's locked from the inside. So, aside from breaking the door down —which I think would be a dead giveaway once he got back—how the hell do you expect us to do that?"

"I thought I told you that already," she said. "I don't have *any* idea! In fact, I was hoping maybe *you'd* have a few suggestions!"

"I'm still not sure I even want to be *involved* in this!" Eric replied, sitting up and spreading his arms. "I know your uncle is a weird guy, but you tell me maybe he's a *killer*!"

All of a sudden, it all made sense to Sabrina. The cross from her parents . . . evil . . . the woman . . . the basement. . . .

"I think he's more than a killer. I think Uncle Viktor is a—a vampire!" she said suddenly.

"Are you crazy?!" Eric asked incredulously.

"Believe her," a soft voice said.

They froze and turned toward the voice to see Jeremy standing about five feet from the breakfast nook, wearing jeans, sneakers, and a plaid shirt with the long sleeves rolled up to his elbows.

"Trust me, Eric," Jeremy said, "you should believe her. She's right about Viktor. But I can fill you in on the rest."

They both stared at him silently for a long time, then turned to each other . . . then looked at him again.

"Fill us in on the rest of *what*?" Sabrina asked.

"I can fill you in on all the things that you couldn't possibly know," Jeremy replied. "Not only you, but everybody *else* around here. I can tell you the *truth*."

He stood there, looking at them, as if waiting to be invited to continue.

"Well, then . . . why don't you sit down," she went on, her voice lowered now, almost to a whisper. "Talk to us."

He did. . . .

"First of all, you're right about Viktor." With his hands folded together Jeremy sat hunched forward at the end of the oval table, his eyes moving back and forth between Sabrina and Eric. "You're right about . . . what he is. And I think you're in danger, Sabrina," he added quietly as he looked at her with sad, dark eyes. "But before we talk about *what* he is, I should tell you *why* he's that way. The story goes back a long . . . *long* time. First of all, Sabrina, Viktor is not your uncle. Your father was raised believing that Viktor was *his* uncle.

That wasn't true, either. Viktor hasn't been anyone's *real* uncle for a very, very long time." He took a deep breath and let it out slowly, then shifted his position in his chair before he began.

"From what I've been able to gather about Viktor," Jeremy said quietly and evenly, "he's somewhere in the neighborhood of two hundred years old, more or less . . . most likely more. Whoever's uncle he *really* was, he or she is long dead. But one thing is certain: Viktor began the family business and went on to acquire what would become the family fortune, and he did it when the country was in its infancy.

"Business was secondary to him, however, a means to an end. Viktor was after only one thing. Power. And, of course, money brings power, so he went after money. He started one of the first shipping companies in the country and made it the biggest—Van Fleet Shipping. But from what I've been able to piece together—and it's taken some time—he didn't do it honestly. He walked over a lot of people. Even killed some people, I think. Just to get what he wanted. Viktor Van Fleet never did an honest or honorable thing in his life. He was evil. And he still is. But he was sin on skates long before he became the monster he is today . . . and that's saying a lot."

Jeremy bowed his head and ran a hand through his hair.

"Sorry," he said. "I'm getting ahead of myself. Viktor used treachery and deceit . . . and, I think, murder . . . the way other businessmen of his time used quill pens, inkwells, and oil lanterns. *They* were the tools of Viktor's trade. But by the time everyone figured out exactly what a horrible man he was, it was too late; he was already too rich and powerful for anyone to do anything about it. He was too big to ignore, and they had to treat him with the deference a man of his position expected and, at that time, was due . . . evil or not."

Jeremy clutched his hands together on the tabletop, so hard that his knuckles became pale and his hands trembled.

"Viktor was so hated," he went on, "that he finally engaged three bodyguards to protect him. In fact, one of those bodyguards took a bullet protecting Viktor from one of his former business partners whom Viktor had gleefully cheated out of a hundred thousand dollars, which was a lot more money back then than it is now. Another bodyguard shot and killed the man before he could get off another shot. But that didn't change anything. The first bodyguard, the one who was shot, took a bullet in the stomach. Viktor refused to pay for a doctor to treat him. He *could* have been saved. But as far as Viktor was concerned, the guy was just doing his job as a bodyguard. As for the bodyguard who shot the would-be assassin . . . well, Viktor did nothing more than buy him a drink. I hope that helps you to understand what kind of man Viktor was back then . . . over two hundred years ago. Because he's had those centuries to get a hell of a lot worse."

Both Sabrina and Eric stared at Jeremy with wide eyes and frozen faces. They looked, in fact, like still photographs, their lips parted, their jaws slack.

"You look shocked," Jeremy said. "I thought you were expecting this sort of thing."

Sabrina slapped her mouth shut and blinked a few times, then said, "Well, yes. At least *I* was expecting it. But at the same time, I'm, uh . . . a little surprised. How do you *know* all this? I mean, *why* do you know all this?"

"I'll get to that in a while," Jeremy said before continuing. "Being the kind of person he was, Viktor was quite lonely back then. He was very rich and very powerful, but he was alone. Until he met a young woman named Chaunte Devareaux. She was eighteen at the time. He was in his midthirties, maybe even late thirties, I'm not sure. But it was the same age he is now. *Physically*, anyway. Being the kind of man he was—a man who got what he wanted when he wanted it—he saw Chaunte and decided he wanted her for himself. Nothing was too good for him, as far as he was concerned . . . not even the most desired young woman in Storm Point—which she *was* at the time, by the way. He had accounts in the finest stores in town and had given her expensive jewelry and trinkets daily. She played hard to get, though, so the chase was on. Each gift was more extravagant than the last and the sentiments in the accompanying cards—always written by a secretary or other assistant—became more lavish, poetic, and forward. And finally, she agreed to meet with him.

"They began to spend a lot of time together. Viktor had Chaunte put on all of his credit accounts in the fanciest shops in Storm Point so she could buy whatever she liked *when*ever she liked. They became the talk of the town. They'd each been talked about a lot already— although no one had anything nice to say about Viktor —but as a couple, they became a kind of royalty. But tongues *really* started wagging once word got out that he'd popped the question and they were to be married. Once everyone realized it was serious, they began to ask one another questions. What could a prominent, wealthy shipping magnate like Viktor Van Fleet want with a peasant like Chaunte Devareaux? She was always courteous and friendly to everyone, but she had no friends that anyone knew of, not even any family in town. In fact, nobody was quite sure where she *lived.*"

"Did they get married?" Sabrina asked. "Viktor and Chaunte?"

Jeremy shook his head slowly. "No, they didn't. And this is where the story gets a little fuzzy. I've tried to learn as much as possible, but there are some things that seem to be out of reach . . . such as the reason Viktor and Chaunte had a falling out. Apparently, he got the idea that she was after his money, that she was a gold digger. Suddenly, he closed himself off to her. He cut off all communications, barred her from his offices, took her name off all his accounts. They were no more. Viktor became rather reclusive for a while . . . but Chaunte completely disappeared. No one knew where she lived, so they certainly didn't know where she'd gone. It was assumed she was distraught, in mourning over the sudden collapse of her relationship with Viktor."

"Did she ever come back?" Eric asked.

"Oh, yes. Unfortunately. If she hadn't, things would

be very different today. Viktor would be long dead, and . . . well, maybe *I* would be alive."

Sabrina and Eric flinched and gawked at Jeremy as if he'd just begun to levitate. Sabrina's mouth worked uselessly for a moment before words finally blurted out:

"What the hell're you *talking* about, Jeremy? If this is a sick joke, or some kind of—"

Jeremy raised both hands to calm her. "I'm sorry. My fault. Forget I said that. At least, for now. I was just getting ahead of myself again, that's all. Okay, now . . . where was I? Oh, yes, Chaunte Devareaux. She *did* come back, but it wasn't what you'd call a social visit. Apparently, she didn't even show her face. She just came long enough to do something to Viktor for dumping her the way he did . . . to get revenge. And boy oh boy, did she get it."

"What did she do?" Eric asked, his voice nearly a whisper.

"Something that has stayed with Viktor to this day," Jeremy said. "She cursed him . . . turned him into a vampire. See, Viktor didn't exactly make the best possible choice for a fiancée. Chaunte Devareaux is a witch. And she's a very powerful one."

They were stunned into silence for a long moment, then Sabrina blinked several times and cocked her head to one side. "You said she . . . *is* a witch?"

Jeremy nodded.

"Then . . . Chaunte Devareaux is . . . still alive?" Eric asked.

Jeremy replied quietly, "That's right."

"Where is she?" Sabrina asked.

"I don't know. For all I know, she's on her way here, if she's not somewhere in Storm Point right now."

Sabrina's eyes widened. "Why would she want to come *here*?"

"Because there is something in this house that she wants. It's the same thing Viktor wants, which is why he was so angry when he learned your dad had changed his will and left everything to you. There's someone else who wants it, too," Jeremy added, taking a deep breath. "*Me*. But, of course, only one of us can have it. And if either Chaunte or Viktor gets it first, we're all in very big trouble."

"But what *is* it?" Sabrina asked impatiently. "What are you *talking* about?"

"The *Black Grimoire*. . . ."

FOURTEEN

The Black Grimoire

As Jeremy held Sabrina and Eric enthralled with his story, the fog thickened around the mansion and over Storm Point as well, turning the night's wet, salty chill into a bone-piercing cold. Beneath the Van Fleet mansion, at the bottom of the hill, Storm Point lay invisible beneath the fog; not even the street lights were able to pierce the murky night. The town was strangely still. Not even the usual sounds of an occasional car starting or a dog barking broke the silence.

It was almost as if the town had fallen under the spell of Jeremy's story, just as Sabrina and Eric had. . . .

Sabrina had made coffee for Eric and herself, and steam rose from the mugs on the table before them. Jeremy paced back and forth in front of the table as he continued.

"Before I start talking about the *Black Grimoire*," he said, "let me go on with the story. Once Viktor realized what had been done to him—that he had been changed, that he was craving blood and could hardly tolerate sunlight—it seems he knew immediately who was responsible for it. Remember, we're talking about a time when people *believed* in witches and were quick to blame them for whatever bad things happened. But I suspect Viktor knew his behavior had hurt Chaunte and that she had a good reason to punish him. So he made arrangements to turn the shipping company over to a brother, then went in search of Chaunte Devareaux."

"Did he know where she'd gone?" Sabrina asked.

"No, but with the same despicable tactics he'd used in his business—along with newly acquired supernatural powers he'd never dreamed of—he made up for that. On the way, he left behind a string of corpses—people he'd tortured for information then killed to get rid of, and others he'd killed for the blood he needed to keep going—until he finally found her. He followed her then, traced her every step, stayed in the shadows, made himself invisible to her and everyone around her, watched every move she made . . . until he finally discovered the secret of her power." Jeremy stopped pacing and faced them, his hands joined behind him. "The *Black Grimoire.*"

After taking a sip of his coffee, Eric asked, with some exasperation in his voice, "Okay, we're back to that, now. Are you going to tell us what it is, or do we play Twenty Questions?"

Jeremy returned to his seat at the table and leaned forward, arms folded, hands clutching his elbows. "It's a book of spells. Well . . . I guess that's not quite accurate, because it's much more than that. It's sort of like a cookbook—an *evil* cookbook—filled with recipes . . .

only these recipes are for curses, and the ingredients are incantations and rituals. The *Black Grimoire* is the *bible* of black magic. There is only one in the whole world because, from what I've been able to learn, it can't be copied."

"Why not?" Sabrina asked.

"The copies disappear. They shrivel up and simply disappear from the hands of whoever tries to copy anything from the book's pages. The book can be read, studied, memorized . . . but never copied. Only a few have ever actually seen the book, and those who have . . . well, let's face it, nobody's memory is perfect. I suppose we should be thankful for that," he muttered, as if to himself. "So, Viktor decided he had to have that book."

"To change himself back?" Eric asked. "I mean, to undo the curse?"

"That might have been his original plan," Jeremy replied. "But remember, Viktor has always craved power more than anything and will do *anything* to *get* it. He'd already proved that in his business dealings. But as a vampire, he had more power than he ever thought possible. *Supernatural* power! There were still things he couldn't do, however; there were weaknesses that held him back. I think Viktor realized quickly that if he had that book, his weaknesses would disappear and he would be able to do anything to anyone. He would be incredibly powerful. Whoever possesses the *Black Grimoire* possesses all the black magic in the world . . . its secrets, its powers. In other words . . . the *Black Grimoire* can make whoever holds it invincible."

There was a long silence at the table as Sabrina and Eric absorbed what they'd been told.

"What about you, Jeremy?" Sabrina asked suddenly. "How do you know all this? How are you *involved*?"

"Well, my involvement began when you were just a little girl, Sabrina. I was visiting for Christmas. Viktor was here as well, but of course we hardly ever saw him . . . and he had no interest in Christmas. I couldn't sleep one night—I think it might have been Christmas Eve—and I settled down in a chair beside the Christmas tree to do a little reading. That's when I heard Viktor come in with someone, a woman, apparently drunk, from the sound of her. He kept trying to quiet her down, *shush*ing her all the time. Their voices faded and I realized he'd gone down the hall toward the basement. With her. I wondered why, because he had his own room. I followed them down the basement stairs quietly and . . . I saw what he did. I heard the horrible noise he made as he sucked the blood from her. I watched her go limp, then finally drop to the floor when he was through."

Jeremy's voice had become thick and emotional with the memory and he paused a moment. "I was terrified and furious at the same time, but what could *I* do? Nothing. So I started back up the stairs, trying to be quiet, but I heard him say, 'Jeremy, my boy . . . come down here and let's talk.' I looked down at him . . . at his eyes . . . and I could do nothing . . . *nothing* but what he told me. I went down the stairs, but we didn't talk, exactly. He was angry and he called me a lot of foul names, then began to speak a language I didn't understand as he pressed a big hand down on the top of my head. Then he opened his mouth wide and threw himself forward, stabbing his fangs into my neck . . . and began to suck my blood." Jeremy stood and began to pace, but slowly now. "When he was finished, he laughed and laughed, with my blood all over his mouth, and said he'd made me exactly like him."

"*Why?*" Sabrina exclaimed.

Eric said, "So you wouldn't tell anyone, right? Because if you were like him—a vampire—you wouldn't just be giving *him* away, you'd be giving *yourself* away, right?"

Jeremy nodded slowly. "That's what he said at first. But that was only part of it. 'Now we are the same, Jeremy,' he said. 'After all, we *are* family, correct? And soon, all of the Van Fleets will be like us. Our family name will not only carry the weight and power of fortune, but the power of eternal life as well. And more . . . so much more. We will be feared. We will be treated as gods. And I will be the patriarch of the Van Fleet family. You see, Jeremy, I have passed on to you my legacy, the legacy of the Van Fleet family. But you are only the first. All the others will follow. And then we will have more than just the servants working in this house to answer our beck and call . . . we will have the world.' " Jeremy swallowed a few times and ran a hand through his hair. "He let me go then. I was sort of in a daze. And . . . I've been this way ever since."

Sabrina's face had turned a sickly pale as she stared at Jeremy. "That's why you haven't changed a bit since I saw you last," Sabrina whispered. After Jeremy nodded in response, she said, in an even softer whisper, "And that's what Viktor meant when he said I was next in line."

Eric leaned toward her with an urgent look on his face as Jeremy returned to his seat, frowning.

"What do you mean?" Jeremy asked. "Next in line for what?"

"The family legacy. He said I was next in line for it, but he wouldn't tell me what it was because it was supposed to be a surprise for my birthday."

"When is your birthday?" Jeremy asked.

"Day after tomorrow."

Eric looked at Sabrina fearfully. "That's why Viktor told me to stay away from you."

"What?" she asked. "When did he tell you that?"

"When do you think? That's why I faked being sick. He didn't just *tell* me to stay away from you . . . it sounded more like a warning. He said he wanted me out of the way so you could carry on the family tradition, something like that." He turned to Jeremy and asked, "What did you mean earlier when you said Sabrina was in danger?"

"Well, I wasn't positive at first, but considering what Viktor said to each of you, I am now. Viktor intends to make you like him. Like *us*. But there's one thing I didn't mention. Viktor made me a vampire . . . but I'm not nearly as powerful as he is. For one thing, he still remembers a lot of what he read in the *Black Grimoire*. For another, he had no *intention* of making me as powerful as he is. I am his underling. And . . . you will be, too. That's what he wants . . . others who are like him, but who aren't as powerful. When he said he was going to be the 'patriarch' of the family, he *meant* it."

"What can we do to stop him?" Sabrina asked.

"Find the *Black Grimoire*. It's somewhere in the house."

"*What*?" Sabrina snapped, almost shooting to her feet. "What the hell is it doing in *here*? Did Mom and Dad know about—"

"Do you remember when your dad had a lot of work done to the house?" Jeremy interrupted. "It was back when you were really little."

The memory of men in overalls moving throughout the house causing a racket with all their hammering, sawing, and drilling came back to her clearly. "Yes."

"Well, he wasn't just adding onto the house or replacing old plaster like he said. He was looking for the *Black Grimoire*. Ever since what Viktor did to me, some things have become pretty clear. You've noticed, I'm sure, that things were always pretty tense between Viktor and your parents, especially your dad. Well, think about it, Sabrina. Remember I said Viktor wants a family of vampires he can control? I think he's *always* wanted that, and I think that's what he wanted to do with your parents. When your dad learned exactly what was going on—when he found out *why* Viktor always seemed so strange and *why* everybody in the family was uncomfortable around him—your dad's discomfort around Viktor became fear."

"That doesn't explain all the work he did on the

house," Sabrina said. "How did he know the book was here?"

"I think Viktor *told* him. I suspect it was the bait Viktor used to get your dad to go along with his plan—power, endless supernatural power."

"But how did the book *get* here?" Eric asked impatiently.

All three of them were talking faster now; their voices took on a certain intensity, as if they suddenly felt they were running out of time or were about to be discovered in a criminal act.

"Viktor was the one who had this house built," Jeremy replied. "He paid for and supervised its design and construction. By the time Viktor had possession of the *Black Grimoire*, he returned to the house. By then, his brother Carl and his family had moved in. He stayed with them awhile, and during his visit it seems he was out of sight, a lot like his stay here, making only obligatory appearances at dinner to say hello to everyone. But what he was *really* doing—I have no proof of this, but I'm willing to bet good money—was studying the *Black Grimoire*. He was committing as much as he could to memory, absorbing as many spells and incantations as he could . . . becoming as powerful as possible. Then he hid the book. He hid it in a place where no one would ever find it, somewhere deep in this house, in a secret place known only to him. He retrieved it at his leisure and pored over it, taking in every bit of information he could. But keep in mind . . . that was nearly two hundred years ago."

"What's that got to do with it?" Sabrina asked.

"Do you know how much work has been done on this house since then?" Jeremy asked, his eyebrows raised high over his eyes. Every ten years or so, someone wanted to change things around. You know, take a wall out and make two rooms into one, or put a wall in and make one room into two. Nearly two hundred years of renovation. This is no longer the same house. It hasn't been for a very long time, in fact. Houses are like people . . . over time, they can change so much that you don't even know them anymore. See what I mean?"

"So why didn't Viktor just take the book out of here if he was in the house all the time?" Sabrina asked.

"Because he *wasn't* in the house all the time. There were a lot of people in the family over the years who couldn't *stand* Viktor, so they never invited him in. And vampires have to be invited into your house before they can enter. Vampires are sort of like, um . . . trouble, I guess. You have to go *looking* for 'em."

"If you don't mind my asking," Eric said coldly, "then how the hell did *you* just barge in here?"

"I was invited into this house years ago by Sabrina's parents. Just like Viktor."

Sabrina said, "So, you think Dad tore the house apart years ago to find the *Black Grimoire* . . . and found it?"

"Yes. After years of Viktor blackmailing your dad with his powers, your father found it. And he left the house to you so Viktor couldn't get to it now. Not *legally*, anyway."

"But why didn't Dad change his will long before this, then? Why did he wait until just before he and Mom were killed?"

Jeremy looked at her for a long time with sad eyes. "Because I think your dad knew they were going to die. I think he knew that Viktor was going to kill them."

Sabrina's mouth dropped open. "B-but *why*?"

"Because Viktor was tired of waiting. He was tired of your parents' resistance to what he wanted, so he did away with them, thinking the entire estate would be left to him. But, of course, he didn't know your dad had changed the will."

"We have to do something," Eric said. "Right away."

"But what?" Jeremy asked.

"Viktor doesn't stay in his room," Sabrina said. "He stays in the basement, doesn't he?"

Slowly, Jeremy nodded.

"We tried to get in there," she said, "but it's locked from the inside."

"You want to go into the basement?" Jeremy asked, smiling. For the first time, they could see his fangs, which curled slightly beneath his upper lip and came to needle points. "We've got time before he gets back. And those locks aren't any trouble for me at all. Let's go. . . ."

FIFTEEN

A Late-Night Interlude

She was a lonely woman who had married at the age of eighteen and had divorced not long after that, thankfully with no children who might have suffered from her unfortunate relationship with a man who turned out to be terribly abusive. Since then, it had become a part of her routine to spend a couple hours each evening in the Silver Dolphin, a dark, smoke-filled bar located on the wooden docks of Storm Point.

Her name was Natalie and she had been sitting on a stool at the bar of the Silver Dolphin for nearly two hours now, making eyes with a very handsome and mysterious-looking man sitting at a small booth in the corner at the end of the bar. She kept giving him her best smile, her sultriest look. Yes, it was dark, but she could tell that he was handsome and, more importantly, *rich*—just the way he sat there in the booth, his back straight and head held high.

Natalie was twenty-two, with long brown hair—although she thought it was a mousy brown—and big dark brown eyes, but people often told her she looked older. Perhaps, she often thought, that was because she spent so much time in the Silver Dolphin, having drink after drink. She had a very thin, girlish figure and she was blessed with skin that gave the impression that she always had a slight tan.

When she'd first noticed the man in the corner booth, she thought he didn't look *too* much older than she, so she'd put forth her best effort to get his attention.

He kept looking at her . . . again and again . . . first nodding toward her . . . then giving her a close-mouthed smile. But it took him nearly two hours to stand up and approach her.

She felt nervous as he came closer, but tried not to lose her smile.

"May I buy you a drink?" he asked in a quiet, deep voice. He wore an odd coat—it looked like a cross between a cape and coat.

"Well," she said, "I'm afraid I've already had a few."

"Then how would you like to take a walk."

Her eyebrows lifted. *"Really?"*

"Yes, really. Shall we go?" He jutted out his elbow, waiting for her to hook her arm in his.

Natalie stood, her smile still fixed on her face, butterflies fluttering in her stomach. "Sure, let's go." She took his arm and they walked out the back door of the Silver Dolphin.

They made small talk—or, rather, *she* did, because he kept her talking while he listened with a gentle smile—as they walked over the wooden planks of the dock, putting more and more space between them and the bar.

He was so attentive, so polite, such a gentleman, that she wasn't at all suspicious when he finally stopped walking.

She glanced back at the Silver Dolphin, only to find that it was nothing more than a glow of light in the distance behind them. When she looked around, Natalie realized there was no one in sight . . . just some boats up ahead of them, tied to the dock.

"By the way," she said, "my name is Natalie. What's yours?"

"My name?" the man asked as he stepped before her and put his hands on her shoulders. He looked directly into her eyes and suddenly Natalie began to feel a bit woozy. Her eyes felt as if they were attached to strings and being tugged, ever so gently, out of their sockets. Mere seconds passed before everything around her— the boats, the dock, the bar behind them—melted like ice cream beneath a hot desert sun.

"My name is not important," the man said quietly, his voice reverberating through her entire body, right down to the marrow of her bones. He pulled her close to him suddenly, but she was not surprised . . . she could not feel *anything*, let alone surprise.

"All that is important," he said, "is that we are together, you and I."

Then he opened his mouth slowly, opened it wide, and she saw, peripherally, the fangs that curled down from beneath his upper lip. But those fangs did not frighten her at all . . . because she could not take her eyes from his.

But then, his eyes disappeared as his face shot forward and the saliva on his fangs glistened slightly . . .

. . . then his fangs stabbed into her neck and her head fell backward limply.

The man began to make wet slurping sounds, sucking sounds, and as Natalie stared up at the cloudy, black night sky, it began to get blacker and blacker and blacker . . . until there was nothing but blackness . . .

. . . and nothingness. . . .

Viktor stepped back away from the splash, then stepped forward to stare down at the black water as it sloshed against the dock. He knew the young woman's body would wander to the bottom and become fishfood. The small anchor he'd found on one of the docked boats would see to that—he'd tied it to her foot with a length of rope he'd bitten off from a coil of rope he'd found on the dock.

Too many had been found, so he'd decided to dispose of all of his victims for a while . . . just as he had the other two earlier tonight. Three all together . . . and they would not be found, he'd seen to that. Once in a while, he might leave one for the police to find—he rather enjoyed watching their futile attempts to track down the killer—but he made sure most of his victims were properly disposed of.

He held his hand out before him and looked at the small, silver locket on the silver chain that he'd taken from around the woman's neck. He carefully put it in his pocket, smiling gently. He always took a keepsake from each victim after feeding; he enjoyed feeling like he still owned a bit of that dead person.

The blood had been good tonight, invigorating. In fact, he was of a mind to take some more from others . . . but he decided against it. He was not tired; he hadn't known weariness for over two hundred years. His life—or, rather, his *un*life—was devoid of things like weariness, pain, loneliness, weakness, sadness, fear; at the same time, it retained the best of his previous life . . . and more, so very much more.

But tonight, he was agitated, preoccupied. No matter how hard he tried to get his mind off it, his thoughts continued to focus on only one thing.

Everything had gone wrong. The will, the estate, that boyfriend of Sabrina's coming back to the house after being warned to the contrary . . . nothing was going as he'd planned. He could not remember the last time he had been in such a bad mood.

Nothing *ever* went wrong for Viktor—he always saw to it. But now it seemed that everything was going wrong in every possible way . . . and he would not *have* it.

Although he was still ready to seek out other victims, Viktor decided he had hunted enough for the night. It was time to go home. . . .

In the Basement

"**I** told you, Jeremy," Sabrina said as they stopped in front of the basement door, "it's locked from the *inside*!"

"And I told *you*, Sabrina, I am not like you. Not at *all*. Remember?"

"Yeah, that's right, you're a—"

They were halfway down the hall to the basement door when Sabrina swallowed her voice and skidded to a halt. When Eric and Jeremy stopped and turned to her, she clutched Eric's elbow and pulled him a step backward with her, away from Jeremy.

"So how do we know," she whispered slowly, "that you won't, um . . . that you aren't going to . . ."

Jeremy smiled. "First of all, Sabrina, I'd never hurt you. I don't feed on people. I refuse to. Viktor and I both need blood, true, but that's where the similarity ends. I feed on the animals around here. And I spend my days in a cave in the cliff face."

Sabrina blinked several times, remembering the cave

she'd seen in the rocky face above the dead deer. "Oh," she said.

"Don't worry," Jeremy assured her warmly. "You're safe."

When they reached the basement door, Jeremy stood facing it. He glanced over his shoulder and said, "Don't let this startle you too much."

Sabrina and Eric stared at him curiously, each of them holding a flashlight.

Suddenly, there was a change in the air, as if it were being shifted by a draft, and Jeremy began to change.

The first thing they noticed—and they saw it simultaneously—was that they could see the basement door . . . *through* Jeremy! He was fading like a ghost, until his body was slowly replaced by a yellowish mist that began to divide into three slender tentacles. The tentacles oozed rapidly into each of the locks, as if they were being sucked through the keyholes by a vacuum cleaner on the other side. The mist was gone in a couple of heartbeats . . . and so was Jeremy.

Sabrina and Eric first looked at each other with shocked expressions, then moved close together, wrapping an arm around each other's waist. Each of them had lost some color in the face.

There were sounds on the other side of the door . . . metallic rattlings . . . solid clicking sounds . . . and the door swung open. Jeremy smiled at them, showing his fangs.

"Told ya," he said jovially.

They stared at him blankly for a long moment, then followed him down the stairs into the dark basement.

"I already tried the light switch," Jeremy said. "It doesn't work. Of course, Viktor doesn't need light, so he probably unscrewed the bulbs."

Sabrina and Eric flicked on their flashlights and the bars of light cut through the dusty air to guide their way down the stairs.

Their feet clattered on the wooden steps as they went lower and lower . . . and finally stopped with soft crunching sounds on the gritty concrete floor at the foot of the stairs. The air was cool and damp, and the darkness was so thick that the flashlight beams didn't get very far.

"What would you like to see first?" Jeremy asked quietly, nearly whispering, as if someone might overhear them.

"I, um, don't know," Sabrina said. "What's . . . *down* here?"

"Well, he keeps souvenirs. I'll show you." Jeremy's footsteps crunched over the concrete as Sabrina and Eric aimed their flashlights straight ahead, the beams cutting through the darkness on each side of Jeremy as they followed him.

The beams scanned one wall of the basement where a number of cardboard and wooden boxes had been stacked. Jeremy went to the wall and opened one of the cardboard boxes, which was stained with age and travel. Sabrina and Eric leaned forward as they shined their lights on the contents.

"Clothes," Eric whispered.

"Women's clothes," Sabrina added, reaching into the box to pull aside the old, crumpled material on top.

"Torn-*up* women's clothes. Real old, too. Falling apart."

Jeremy leaned over and opened another box, this one wooden, and slid aside the lid. It contained several dusty old books on top of which lay a thick manuscript of old, yellowed, dog-eared pages bound together by twine.

The next box was filled with shoes . . . lots of women's shoes, only one of each. There wasn't a complete pair in the lot.

The fourth box held a mass of old jewelry—necklaces, bracelets, rings, earrings, broaches—all of which looked, at first glance, quite real. At second glance, Sabrina realized that a lot of the jewelry *was* quite real! With the jewelry were a few women's evening gloves—again, no pairs, only unmatching singles—and delicate handkerchiefs; the material was old and tattered and dusty.

Sabrina picked up one of the handkerchiefs and held it before her flashlight. It had a broad lace border that had begun to decay from age. And there was something else . . . a dark stain smeared over a strip of the lace border, the color of old rust . . . a dark, reddish-brown. Sabrina touched the stain with a fingertip, brushed it gently, then dropped the handkerchief back in the box.

"That looks like . . . blood," she whispered.

"Why does he have all this stuff?" Eric asked. "It's all women's stuff . . . things he'd never use."

"Like I said," Jeremy replied, "he keeps souvenirs. It's some kinda kink of his. Maybe it makes him feel more in control, or something, I don't know. But he's got boxes and boxes of this stuff. They're stacked all over the place down here," he said with a wave of his hand. "And I think he's got more in storage someplace. But I don't know where. After all, it would take a lot of boxes for two hundred years' worth of souvenirs."

Sabrina turned to him, shining her flashlight downward. "Okay, so we know he stores his memorabilia down here. But does he actually *stay* down here?"

Jeremy turned and pointed upward. "Look at the windows."

Both flashlight beams swept in the direction of his finger and fell on sections of black tarpaulin covering the rectangular, ground-level windows.

"To keep out the sunlight," Jeremy explained as he dropped his arm to his side. "He replaces them regularly to make sure they're in good shape and no light seeps through."

"How long has he been staying down here?" Sabrina asked.

"He's never stayed anywhere else in this house. Whenever he visited, this is where he stayed. That's why your dad put those locks on the outside of the door. It wasn't to keep you kids from hurting yourselves down here . . . it was to keep you from discovering Viktor's bed. Victor added the inside locks for his own purposes."

Eric frowned. "His . . . bed?"

"Sabrina, your dad felt helpless against Viktor. He tried his best to protect you," Jeremy said, then took a few steps away from them, disappearing in the darkness beyond the flashlight beams.

Sabrina and Eric turned and tried to follow him with their flashlights; the glowing beams crossed again and again until they fell on Jeremy's back . . . and the long, rectangular crate that lay before him. They moved forward, staring at the crate. It was in the center of the basement, placed at the very edge of the unfinished concrete floor. Beyond it lay moist, soft dirt.

"This is the crate they were moving in when I got here," Sabrina said with a trembling whisper. "Remember?"

Eric nodded, gulping.

"So, um, what's in the crate, huh, Jeremy?" she asked. "What the hell's in there?"

"What do you *think* is in there, Sabrina?"

"Oh, my God," Eric said hoarsely.

Sabrina's head jerked around to look at him . . . then followed his gaze and the direction of his flashlight.

Eric was staring at the dirt floor beyond the concrete; specifically, he was staring at a freshly dug mound of dirt. The mound was not piled very high, but it was about five and a half feet long . . . and there was a shovel propped against the wall a few feet behind it.

"I was right," Sabrina said, shining her light on the mound as well. "That woman . . . she never left this basement. And that's why."

"Do you want to open this thing or not?" Jeremy asked, as if the new grave in the dirt floor did not surprise him at all.

"Yeah," Eric said, stepping toward the long crate. "Let's get this over with."

He froze suddenly.

Sabrina stiffened.

There was a sound in the darkness . . . a skittering sound that quickly grew louder . . . and closer.

Eric turned to Sabrina and Jeremy with a slack jaw and asked in a breath, "What the hell is—"

He was unable to finish his sentence because the rats were on them in a heartbeat. They flowed over the concrete floor around each end of the crate like a wave washing over a rock on the beach, their tiny claws scratching on the concrete and little eyes and fangs glistening in the flashlight beams as they rushed forward, making shrill screaking sounds as their numbers seemed to grow and grow, as if from nowhere.

Suddenly, Jeremy held both arms out at his side and backed up, forcing Sabrina and Eric backward, away from the rats.

"Get back and *stay* back!" he shouted, pushing them hard with his arms.

Once Sabrina and Eric had backed up all the way to the stairs, Jeremy took two broad steps toward the rats and leaned forward with his knees bent, hands on his thighs and elbows jutting out on each side. He glared down at the rats moving over the floor toward him as he leaned very slowly to the right, then to the left, turning his head even more slowly, moving his eyes over the swarm of rats . . .

. . . and he growled. It was the fierce growl of a vicious, wild animal—the kind of growl Sabrina had heard from downstairs on her first night home—and it sent gooseflesh over the backs and arms of both Sabrina and Eric.

A silence fell over the basement. In the glow of their downward-aimed flashlights, Sabrina and Eric saw the rats come to a complete halt . . . all of them at once.

Very slowly, Jeremy stood up straight, his head still bowed low and moving back and forth slowly. He growled again, this one quiet and low. He raised his arms at his sides and waved the rats backward.

They remained still for a long moment there on the floor, then, slowly, the rats began to move back. They did not turn around and go back into the refuge of the darkness . . . they *backed up*! Each of the rats had its pointy head turned upward toward Jeremy as it began to back away, tiny fangs now hidden beneath closed snouts, tiny eyes never leaving Jeremy's face.

In moments, they were gone . . . dissolved into the darkness from which they had come so suddenly.

Jeremy turned to them and said, "I'm sorry. I should have expected that. See, um . . . vampires can control lower forms of life. Rats, wolves, dogs, that sort of thing. Even cockroaches, believe it or not." He smiled, and even though his fangs showed and glimmered in the glow of the flashlights, they could not detract from the warmth of his apologetic smile. "I'm sorry that you had to, um . . . well, I'm sorry for the scare. But they're gone now. And they'll stay gone, I promise. So. Do you want to open this thing, or what?"

As she and Eric moved forward, Sabrina pulled at the chain around her neck until the cross flopped onto her chest outside her sweatshirt. She held it between her thumb and forefinger and rubbed it gently, as if it might protect her . . . but of course it was only a piece of jewelry and could do nothing more than hang from her neck.

They moved toward Jeremy—and the long crate—slowly, their flashlights shining before them. Suddenly, Sabrina stopped as she held her cross, her eyes on Jeremy.

"Um, I don't know if I should have this with you around," she said quietly, almost apologetically.

"Have what?" Jeremy asked.

"This cross around my neck."

He chuckled briefly. "Sabrina, I was raised in a devoutly religious home and used to go to church every week. So, in spite of my, uh, *current* state . . . my faith is still intact. I feel no differently about the cross and its significance than I ever did. Viktor, on the other hand, has always despised religion and all that comes with it. *His* reaction to the cross would be altogether different from mine. So, don't worry about me. I'm sort of . . . well, I guess you could say I'm *immune* to the effects of the cross. Just keep garlic away from me. It's like a very bad allergic reaction for those of us who are, um . . . like me. No exceptions."

Sabrina smiled and continued forward with Eric as Jeremy turned away from them, leaned forward, and slid the top off the long crate. They stopped at the crate and shined their flashlights into it.

Inside the crate lay a shiny oak casket. The lid was split across the middle, so that only the top could be opened . . . or only the bottom, if that's what you wanted.

"He's not in there, is he?" Eric asked fearfully.

"Of *course* not," Jeremy said cheerfully. "He's out . . . painting the town red, so to speak."

"Can we open it?" Sabrina asked.

Smiling, Jeremy stepped in front of them, reached down and lifted both sections of the casket's lid.

The casket was lined with fine white satin and had a pillow at the head. And it was, indeed, empty.

As she stared into the casket, Sabrina began to stroke her cross again, almost frantically, tugging on the chain without even realizing it. Suddenly, the chain's latch broke, the cross slipped from her fingers and fell onto the cushioned, silk-lined bed of the casket.

There was a sharp hissing sound then, and tendrils of thick yellow smoke began to curl up toward them. It happened so quickly that the greasy yellow smoke had reached them by the time Sabrina even realized the chain had fallen from her neck . . . or that the thick tentacles of smoke were coming from around the edges of her own cross, which lay in the casket.

The smell was awful, horrible . . . a mixture of sulphur and rotting meat. And the hissing sound grew louder as the cross began to sink into the cushion, as if it were melting its way through the silk and everything beneath it.

"My *God*!" Sabrina blurted. "What's happening?"

Jeremy said, "I told you the cross would affect Viktor. It also affects everything that is closely connected to him . . . like his resting place."

Jeremy leaned forward and began to reach into the casket for the cross, when the sound of shattering glass cut through the darkness like a knife and something ripped through the black tarpaulin.

Sabrina's back stiffened and she gasped loudly.

Eric aimed his flashlight at the broken window and torn tarpaulin. When the sound of flapping wings shot through the silence in the basement, he jerked the beam of light around to find the source.

"Oh my God," Jeremy said.

The flashlight beam fell on a winged creature that continued to fly rapidly back and forth, back and forth in the basement. It had a wingspan of about three feet, and the wings moved so fast that they were nearly a blur . . . like a very large bat.

Sabrina slapped a hand onto Jeremy's arm and clutched tightly. "What, oh my God *what*?" she hissed.

After a long moment filled with the sound of the creature's flapping wings, Jeremy said, "It's Viktor. . . ."

SEVENTEEN

A Confrontation
with Viktor

The enormous bat dropped to the concrete floor in a dark heap, its long wings spread full. It remained still for a moment, then it began to tremble . . . then convulse . . . then something rose up out of the creature's middle in a liquidy blur, something black and tall and undefined. The bat's wings shrank quickly, until they were gone . . . and yet they were *not* gone. The tall, dark figure that stood where the bat, just a heart-beat ago, had been lying, spread the wings out at each side, until they disappeared silently, like shadows across a window.

The figure took three steps forward as Sabrina, Eric, and Jeremy huddled close together, until it moved into the glow of the flashlights and became clearly visible.

The cape of Viktor's Inverness coat fluttered around his shoulders and upper arms like an echo of those wings that had disappeared just a moment before. His upper lip pulled back over his razor-sharp fangs and he released a long, wet, vicious hiss as his head craned forward.

"I am very curious to know," he said slowly, his voice low, nearly a growl, "what the three of you are doing down here. After all, this is nothing more than a basement. What could possibly attract you to this subterranean rat's nest?"

None of them moved or spoke, but they did not shrink beneath his piercing gaze.

Viktor's eyes turned to Sabrina and he took two very slow steps forward, smiling ever so slightly. "Sabrina, my dear Sabrina . . . you are making such a horrible mistake. Aren't you, my dear? You know it . . . you can feel it, can you not?"

Eric turned his head slowly to look at Sabrina. Her face was slack and blank as she stared up at Viktor, who moved closer and closer, very slowly, his eyes locked onto hers as he towered over her.

Jeremy shot forward, stepping in front of Sabrina to confront Viktor with a stern face.

"Stay away from her, Viktor. I've stood by and watched you do a lot of things. I've let a lot of stuff pass. But not this. If you want to get to Sabrina, you'll have to go through me."

Viktor's eyes widened slightly as he looked at Jeremy, then his eyebrows rose and the corners of his mouth turned up in a smirk. From deep in his chest, a distorted laugh rose and was burped out through open lips.

"You must be joking, Jeremy," he said as he slapped a hand on Jeremy's face, dug his fingers into the skin and lifted him about eighteen inches off the floor . . . by his face. Viktor continued: "Because you know as well as I do, Jeremy, that you are no threat to me."

Staring up at Jeremy as he held him up high with a stiff arm, Viktor began to speak a bizarre, babbling language. Then he stopped, remained frozen there for a moment, then threw Jeremy to the side like a light piece of trash.

Jeremy disappeared into the darkness at the other end of the basement and fell to the moist dirt with a thud.

Viktor moved a step closer to Sabrina.

Eric suddenly moved forward and shouted, "I don't know what the hell you think you're doing, but whatever it is, you're not gonna get away with—"

Viktor swept his arm outward, as casually as if he were swatting at a fly, and the back of his hand hit Eric in the chest.

Eric felt his feet leave the ground as his breath left his lungs. He tumbled through the air, head over heels, then hit the concrete hard and rolled like a stuntman until he slammed into the side of the crate that contained Viktor's casket. He opened his mouth wide and sucked at the air, trying to breathe again, his hands clutching his chest, until air finally began to gush into his lungs.

Even above his gasps for air, Eric could hear Viktor's voice, and he turned his head toward it to see what was happening.

"It's not your birthday," Viktor said as he stepped toward Sabrina, "but that is not important. What *is* important is that you receive the family legacy. Right now. After all . . . what's the point of waiting?"

Eric watched as Viktor placed his hands on each side

of Sabrina's head. He knew, after what Jeremy had told them, what Viktor had in mind: he was about to do to Sabrina what he'd done to Jeremy. And Eric wasn't about to let him get away with it.

Shooting to his feet, Eric leaned over the edge of the crate and into the casket. Amidst a blackened, burned section of silk lay Sabrina's cross and chain. Eric reached down, grabbed it, then spun around and headed quickly toward Viktor.

"You will thank me for this later," Viktor was saying to a bedazzled Sabrina as he placed a large hand atop her head. He began to speak once again in that alien tongue as Eric used his thumb to press the small cross to the base of Viktor's skull hard, *very* hard.

The hissing sound began immediately as tendrils of yellow smoke began to curl from around the cross and the smell of burning hair began to spread around them. The smoke was followed by flames that burst suddenly and silently out from under the cross, singeing Viktor's dark hair.

Then, as Viktor fell backward away from Sabrina, there came the scream. It was a horrible scream, but Eric moved backward with Viktor, still holding the small cross to the base of his skull . . .

. . . until Viktor spun around to face Eric. His eyes were practically bulging and his mouth was open wide. The yellow smoke still curled upward from the back of his head.

Eric held the cross before him in his right hand, his arm stiff as he stumbled backward, and Viktor raised his arms and covered his eyes with them. Viktor hissed again, but more viciously this time, as he staggered sideways.

"Get the hell *out* of here!" Eric shouted, "*Away* from us! *Now!*"

Viktor lunged toward Eric and let loose a horrible growl, but in the blink of an eye, he melted into the large bat that had plunged through the window earlier. The wings flapped endlessly as the creature flew in frantic, rapid circles in the basement, trailing the sickly smelling yellow smoke . . . then shot out the window as suddenly as it had shot into it, leaving behind a dead, funereal silence.

Sabrina stood in place, her body as stiff as a mannequin's, her wide eyes staring intensely at the space that had been occupied by Viktor only a moment before.

Eric turned to her at the very second she collapsed to the floor.

"Jeremy!" he called as he rushed to her side, kneeling beside her. "Jeremy, where *are* you? Can you *hear* me? C'mon, man, I need some *help* here!"

Just as Sabrina began to stir, there were sounds of movement in the darkness, then Jeremy said, in a hoarse voice, "I'm coming . . . I'm coming."

He staggered out of the darkness with half-open eyes and joined Eric at Sabrina's side. He picked up Sabrina's flashlight and with the strength of both of them —Eric and Jeremy—they led her, staggering drunkenly, up the stairs and into the hallway outside the basement door.

It was with great pleasure that Eric closed the basement door behind them and locked it. . . .

EIGHTEEN

A Plan

Jeremy made some tea while Eric sat with his arm around Sabrina in the breakfast nook. Sabrina was confused and her eyes looked bleary and unfocused, but she was coming around.

"My God, whuh-what . . . what happened?" she asked, blinking at Eric.

"Well, what happened was that you, um . . . you were nearly given the family legacy."

She rubbed her eyes, then her temples, groaning quietly as Jeremy placed a cup of hot, strong tea in front of her, then took a seat on the other side of the table. She leaned toward the table with a sigh, placing a hand on her chest. Then her back stiffened. Her hand patted her chest, then moved up to her neck, feeling for the chain.

"I've got it right here," Eric said, placing the cross and chain on the table. "It pretty much saved our butts."

She placed her hand gently over the cross, then looked at Eric and asked, "What happened?"

He told her. When he was finished, Sabrina sipped her tea.

"What're we gonna do?" she asked, her words still slurring a bit.

"We're going to have to find the *Black Grimoire*," Jeremy said. "It's somewhere in this house."

Suddenly, Eric looked very enthusiastic as he turned to Jeremy. "You can help us! Like you did with the locks! You could, could, um . . . well, *mist* your way through the walls of this house in no time."

"You think I haven't tried?"

"Then where is it?" Sabrina asked.

"I don't know. I only know it's hidden somewhere in this house, hidden well. Chances are, the best way to find it would be to tear the house apart."

"You know how long that would take?" Eric asked.

"Not if we had help," Sabrina said. She turned to Eric. "What about Steve and Chanelle and Janna . . . and Rob and Cheri?"

"Are you kidding?" Eric said with a chuckle. "What would we *tell* them?"

"Well, we couldn't tell them the truth, but . . . we could tell them *something*."

He thought about it a moment. "We should go see them tomorrow, then. They've all got jobs down at the mall. I don't know if they're all working tomorrow, but we can try."

"First thing in the morning," Sabrina said, her voice and eyes clearer now.

"Yeah, first thing," Eric said, glancing at the clock on the wall. "I should get home, then. Get some sleep."

Sabrina's eyes widened in panic as she wrapped her

arms around him and held him close. "Oh no, don't! Please don't go, Eric! I don't want to be alone."

Very quietly, Jeremy stood and slowly began to walk away from the table. "I'll leave you two alone now," he said. "I've got some things to do. I'll see you tomorrow evening."

By the time Sabrina and Eric turned toward him, Jeremy was gone.

"I know it's late and it's a hassle, and everything," Sabrina said. "But I'm scared to death, Eric. You're all I've got and I don't want you to go away. I'm just too . . . well, I'm too scared that if you go away, you won't come back."

They looked into each other's eyes for a long time, then the space between their faces began to close as they leaned together, their lips meeting.

The kiss was long and passionate, as if it might be their last . . .

. . . because after what happened in the basement, they both knew it might *very well* be their last. . . .

NINETEEN

Aunt Caroline's Arrival

The next morning, over breakfast, Eric and Sabrina discussed the various ways they could approach their friends with the problem at hand. They couldn't come right out and tell them the truth without being laughed out of the mall. First, they agreed to call their friends right after breakfast and see if their work schedules would allow them all to get together that afternoon for lunch. Then they agreed on a story: at the reading of her parents' will, Sabrina learned that a family heirloom was hidden somewhere in the structure of the house, and they were going to need help with some reverse carpentry to find it. It was a pretty vague story, but they thought they might get away with it if they glossed over the finer details.

The night before, Eric had called his parents to let them know he was staying at Sabrina's, then the two of them sat in front of the television, holding each other close. They spent a lot of time kissing until, finally, they fell asleep with MTV playing quietly in front of them. Now they were tired and achy, but enthusiastic about the task ahead of them. Elsa scolded them for not getting a good night's sleep, and threatened not to feed them at all; but, of course, she did.

When they finished breakfast, they stood from the table, both yawning contagiously. They headed for the stairs to go up to Sabrina's room and call their friends, each with an arm around the other's waist, their heads leaning together wearily. As they were passing the foyer, the front door opened and they froze, turning to the door to see Hans entering with a large suitcase in each hand. Behind him, carrying another suitcase and a vanity case, was Aunt Caroline.

Her eyes wide with surprise, Sabrina hurried to her aunt and gave her a big hug, making her drop the cases at her sides.

"Aunt Caroline, it's so good to see you!" she exclaimed, taking a step back to get a good look at the woman.

She was plump, with short black hair that glittered with streaks of silver and a round, warm face that still opened in the same broad smile Sabrina remembered from her childhood.

"My goodness," Aunt Caroline said, her hands on Sabrina's shoulders, "you're *so beautiful*! Your mother had sent pictures, but they didn't do you justice."

They chatted quietly for a while there in the foyer, then Sabrina introduced Eric, who shook Aunt Caroline's hand.

"You mean the same Eric who used to chase squirrels with you in the backyard when I came to visit?" she asked. When Sabrina nodded, Aunt Caroline clicked her tongue, shook her head and said, "My, my. Everyone's growing up behind my back."

Eric took the suitcases from Hans and he and Sabrina showed Aunt Caroline to her room upstairs. When she mentioned how hungry she was, Sabrina told her to go down and get some breakfast. Once she was gone, they headed for Sabrina's room.

"Jeez," Sabrina whispered, "I forgot she was coming."

"What do you think she's gonna make of all this?" Eric asked.

She sighed heavily as they went into her room. "I really don't know." She sat on the edge of her bed. "We should probably just keep quiet about it for now."

Eric agreed with a nod.

"So," Sabrina said, "who should we call first?"

TWENTY

At the Mall

The Seabreeze Mall was situated on the northern end of Storm Point and, with the surrounding parking lots included, sprawled over nearly ten acres of land. Towering above it from the very center of the mall's structure was an enormous sign that read SEA-BREEZE MALL in neonlike letters, rotating slowly in the year-round mist that blanketed the area.

Sabrina and Eric had arranged to meet with their friends in the Seabreeze Eatery, a small diner inside the mall. When they entered the diner, they realized they were the last to arrive, because the others were already laughing and talking around a table in the corner.

They had known one another since first grade, and although Sabrina had been gone for a while, she'd been careful to keep in touch with them, and as a result of all those letters and phone calls, she had a pretty good idea what had been going on in her friends' lives. And yet, seeing them again made her realize how much time had passed since they'd all been together, and she rushed to the table, followed by Eric, her eyes a little misty. As a result, they spent a good deal of time at the table exchanging hugs and talking and laughing. Everyone extended their condolences to Sabrina, but that did not dampen the excitement and enthusiasm between Sabrina and her friends.

There were five of them, all different, but with just enough in common to have stuck together for all those years.

Janna Freed was very thin with golden hair that was styled in a perfect wedge, and a face and body one would expect to see on the cover of *Y.M.* or *Sassy*. She had always been popular in school because of her bright, outgoing personality; her popularity had grown in high school because of her beauty, and she'd been elected the president of three different clubs—photography, debate, and social—as well as the editor of the yearbook. There was never a shortage of dates for Janna, of course, and she chose to play the field, dating one guy after another, rather than settling with one boyfriend.

Chanelle Duryea was a tall, attractive black girl with a laugh that carried for a good distance. She was very athletic and was captain of the swimming and gymnastic teams. Unlike Janna, whose grades were average, Chanelle excelled in every class, and nearly everyone had, at one time or another, turned to her for help with their studies.

Seated beside Chanelle was Rob Peters. The two of them were very close because they had something in common: everyone came to them for help with their homework. Rob's frizzy black hair was as wiry as his thin, bony body. The smoke-gray wire frames of his glasses were in style, but the lenses were very thick and made his dark brown eyes look owlish. In fact, the frames of his glasses were the only thing about him that were stylish. His hair was unmanageable, and his clothes were a bit less than current; he was the eldest of three kids in a single-parent family, and even though his mother's job in a nearby plastics factory did provide enough money to afford fashionable new clothes, Rob just didn't care about his appearance. But Rob knew a little bit about everything and had a wit sharp enough to cut through wood, and everyone in the group was devoted to him.

Especially devoted to Rob was Cheri Scotch, who loved his sharp wit. They were only friends, but they were so close that a casual observer might think otherwise. Back in grammar school, Cheri had been an ugly duckling and boys and girls alike had made fun of her. Had it not been for her group of friends, all of whom stood up for her like soldiers, she might have drawn inward and become a wallflower, a silent, down-looking misfit. But now, things were different. She was a lovely, voluptuous redhead, with an abundant head of hair that fell halfway down her back and a figure that turned heads wherever she went. She was outgoing and had few social inhibitions, and she gave most of the credit for that to her supportive friends. She had a sense of humor that could find a joke in the darkest of subjects, and which tended to be off-color. She had dated for a while, seeing guy after guy, like Janna. Then she'd found one, linked up with him and had been terribly hurt, so hurt that she wouldn't even talk about the details with her friends. Now she preferred to go out with her friends, or groups of people.

Steve Brooks was a very muscular young man who spent a lot of time in the weight room. He had short blond hair and bright blue eyes with pale brows and lashes. Steve was the kind of guy who would, under usual circumstances, be called a "jock" at any high school in the country. But along with his all-American good looks, he had a severe lisp. It had been the target of endless painful teasing during grammar school, but even in high school, the teasing hadn't stopped. Like Cheri, he'd taken refuge in his group of friends, and was now inseparable from them. Unfortunately, he'd spent so much time in the weight room to buff up and compensate for his lisp that he'd spent little time studying. His grades had always been on the low side, and like so many others, he'd gone to Chanelle and Rob for help. While they sometimes turned down others for lack of time, they always had time to help out their friend.

They ordered their food as they continued to talk, until the conversation finally worked its way around to Sabrina.

"You said this was important," Rob said.

"Yeah," Chanelle added, "you said you had to talk to us as soon as possible, right away, so . . . here we are. What's going on?"

Sabrina wasn't sure how to start and she turned to Eric as all the others stared at her. Finally, Sabrina began to tell the story that she and Eric had fabricated. Everyone listened silently as she spoke, and when she was finished, a long silence followed.

For a moment, Sabrina thought she was about to be refused by all of them as they stared at her with blank expressions, and she glanced at Eric—who looked as if he were thinking the same thing—then said, "I'll pay you. For your work, I mean," she added. "Look . . . everything is mine now, right? So, if you help us with this, I'll pay you money."

They still remained silent, looking uncertain as they stared at her.

"Okay, tell you what," she said. "If you help us out, I'll not only pay you money . . . I'll see to it you get a better meal than you could get in the best restaurant in town. Whatever you want, you name it, spaghetti, lasagna, chicken, ham, a complete turkey dinner, Chinese food or—"

"Okay, okay," Janna said, holding up a palm. "I think we get the idea. You're pretty desperate for the help, right?"

Sabrina nodded.

"But what exactly will we be *looking* for?" Steve asked.

"Well, um, uh . . . um . . ." Sabrina didn't know what to say and turned to Eric for help.

"It's a book," Eric said. "A very old book. It's worth, um, a lot of money, y'know? I mean, it's really, really old. And it's somewhere in the structure of the house."

Rob frowned and scratched his head, then adjusted his glasses. "Not that I'm casting aspersions on your parents, Sabrina," he said, "but how in the world could anyone *possibly* lose something in the *walls* of a *house*?"

At that point, Eric and Sabrina looked at each other

for help. Finally, Sabrina decided to use some of the information given to them by Jeremy: "Well, see, the house is nearly a couple hundred years old. This particular book was hidden within the house way back then and, well, y'know, there's been a lot of work done on the house since then. I mean, all those years you've gotta figure the house isn't the same house it *used* to be, right?"

Everyone around the table looked at each other for a moment, exchanging glances. After a while, Steve said, "Well, I don't have any plans for tonight."

"Neither do I," Janna said.

They all agreed; there were no plans for that night.

Finally, Cheri said, "Well, I don't think we'll take your money. But as far as I'm concerned, that spaghetti feed you mentioned sounds real good." She smiled as she reached over and clutched Sabrina's hand. . . .

TWENTY-ONE

Awakenings

Deep in the cave that cut downward into the cliff side behind the Van Fleet mansion, Jeremy began to awaken slowly after the setting of the sun. He was hanging upside down from the curved ceiling of a small, narrow branch of the cave in the shape of a three-foot-long bat. He had not taken that shape because he enjoyed it; it was just that hanging from a crooked stalactite was much more comfortable than curling up on rock in his human form.

Once he was awake, he blinked several times, stretched his wings wide and licked his lips with his tiny black tongue.

Tomorrow was Sabrina's birthday. The sun had just gone down, so there was little time before that day arrived. He knew that Viktor would consider any time after midnight to be her birthday, so once the clock struck twelve, Sabrina would be in more danger than ever . . . in danger of receiving the "family legacy."

Jeremy knew he would have to feed before he went into the house, because he had a job before him; he had to protect Sabrina from Viktor Van Fleet. . . .

* * *

In the basement beneath the Van Fleet mansion, Viktor opened his eyes in the darkness of his closed casket.

He had fled the basement earlier because of Sabrina's cross. He had come back, however, after the three of them had left the basement, because his casket was his bed and Viktor needed his sleep . . . especially right around dawn, just before the sun rose.

But now the sun had set again and it was the beginning of a new night. And Viktor knew that, as of midnight, Sabrina would be seventeen . . . it was her birthday . . . and he was determined to take her on her birthday.

After all, he was the father of the Van Fleet family, the *creator* of the Van Fleet *fortune*! Shouldn't he be able to decide the future of the Van Fleet family? Especially considering that he was not only its father, but also still around to determine its future.

And as Viktor saw it, the future of the Van Fleet family encompassed a family of people who, like him, were immortal and would be able to serve under him as he eventually gained control of town after town . . . state after state . . . and eventually much, much more than that . . .

. . . but he knew he could not do that until he retrieved the *Black Grimoire*.

Viktor intended to find that book. In fact, he suspected that Sabrina and her young friend Eric— the rebellious little rat who had defied Viktor's orders—

might be instrumental in *helping* him to find that book.

He lifted his arms, pressed his palms to the bottom of the casket's lid and pushed upward.

It was the beginning of a new night. . . .

TWENTY-TWO

The Destruction Begins

They arrived in two different cars—Chanelle's and Steve's—and entered the house enthusiastically, ready to go to work, although they were more than willing to say that they had no idea what the hell they were doing.

An hour earlier, Sabrina and Eric had talked about where they should start. They came to the conclusion that they had no idea . . . but they'd decided on the library. After all, it was filled with shelves of books that were visible . . . so perhaps there was a book some-where in the room that was *not* visible.

With the rich smell of spaghetti sauce in the air, they went to the library and went to work.

First, they removed books from their shelves, stack-ing them on the floor in the middle of the room in no particular order. As each bookcase was emptied, they removed it from the wall and began to dismantle that wall with the help of tools Sabrina had brought from the utility closet.

It pained her to see the library—her favorite room in

the house—being torn up so brutally . . . but she also knew it was necessary.

To hell with all the sentimentality, she thought. *This is more important. Much more important.*

It was noisy and unpleasant, but as each bookcase was moved, the wall behind it was immediately under attack; the clawed ends of hammers smacked and crunched through the cream-colored wallpaper and the plaster was torn away a chunk at a time.

They continued to dismantle the library for nearly three hours, until Cheri rose to her feet, leaned backward with two fists pressing into her lower back, and said, "Okay, so we've been tearing this place apart for quite a while, right?" She straightened up, ran a hand through her red hair and said, "I think we deserve a break at the *very* least!"

"Okay, you're right," Sabrina said. "I'm sure Elsa's got the spaghetti ready. Let's go out there and eat . . . as long as you guys are willing to get back to this when we're done."

"After a spaghetti dinner?" Steve asked with a look of genuine disdain on his face. "What, are you *kidding*?"

Sabrina sighed, her hands, forearms, and face splotched with plaster dust. "Do you want to eat or not?"

They all got to their feet and headed toward the door, their voices blending in mutual agreement.

Sabrina was surprised to find that Elsa had already set the table, as if she'd been waiting for them to decide to come out and eat. But as everyone was taking a seat at the dining-room table, she realized there was a potential stumbling block. She turned to Eric—the only one who had not yet seated himself—and gave him a wink as she headed into the kitchen to find Elsa.

"Has Aunt Caroline eaten yet, Elsa?" Sabrina asked.

"Almost two hours ago. She retires early, you know. And you could take a lesson from your aunt Caroline, I think. This business of staying up all hours with your friends and eating so late is—"

Sabrina interrupted her: "Thank you, Elsa. I have to get back to dinner."

She sat beside Eric, and while the others were wolfing down their spaghetti and taking great bites of their garlic bread, Sabrina realized that she and Eric were hardly touching their food. It was almost as if they were waiting for something bad to happen, something that would get in the way of their plan and prevent them from finding the *Black Grimoire*.

That something bad began a few minutes into the dinner.

"I still don't get it," Rob said. "Even though we're doing this—and don't get me wrong, Sabrina, I'm happy to help you out—I don't get *why* we're doing this. I mean, we're looking for an old book, right? But I still don't understand exactly why this old book is hidden somewhere within the walls of this house."

"I'm sorry, Sabrina, but he's right," Janna said as she took a bite of garlic bread. She chewed for a moment before speaking again. "This whole thing seems a little odd, like, um . . . well, like something's missing."

"Yeah," Steve said. "Why would somebody hide a book in a wall, huh?"

Cheri leaned back in her chair, shrugged her shoulders and said, "Look, this is a priceless heirloom we're looking for, right?" She leaned forward again, placing her elbows on the table and the knuckles of her locked fingers beneath her chin. "So if you're going to hide something priceless, you might as well hide it *deep*, right? Okay. So, I don't have any problem with this thing at all. As far as I'm concerned, we're just looking for a priceless heirloom that somebody hid really well." She turned to Sabrina with raised eyebrows and a big smile. "Am I right . . . or am I right?"

Laughter burst from Sabrina's mouth suddenly—laughter that came from relief and gratitude—and she slapped a hand over her mouth. Finally, she said, "Oh, boy, are you right, Cheri. You're so right, I could *kiss* you!"

"Hey," Cheri said, "don't get carried away with yourself, okay? I'm just saying what I think."

"Well, you're thinking right," Sabrina said, her voice full of enthusiasm as she turned to Eric. "Isn't she? She's right, right?"

Eric loosened up a bit, smiled and nodded. "Yeah, Cheri's right."

They went on with their dinner. Even Sabrina and Eric began to dig in, knowing that they had achieved the desired effect on the others. They all took their time, because they knew that when they were done, it was back to work in the library . . . back to tearing the place apart to find an old book about which they knew nothing. . . .

TWENTY-THREE

Enter Jeremy and Aunt Caroline

Everyone was working busily when Sabrina excused herself to go to the bathroom. One second after she closed the library door behind her, Jeremy said quietly, "Exactly what do you two think you're doing, anyway?"

Sabrina gasped, startled at first, then hissed, "What do you *think* we think we're doing? We're trying to find that damned *book!*"

"But what did you tell your friends? I've been watching all of you, y'know. Through the gap between those drapes over the window."

"We didn't tell them the truth, if that's what you're worried about."

"No, it's not. What I'm worried about is that tomorrow's your birthday and Viktor has some very specific *plans* for you. Those plans might have failed down in that basement, but believe me, they won't fail on your birthday . . . not once Viktor has set his mind to seeing them through."

"Why do you think we've asked our friends to help

us?" she whispered frantically. "Because we want to find the *Black Grimoire!*"

"But you don't have long. Come midnight, it's your birthday, and that's less than three hours away, Sabrina! This is a big house—bigger than *three hours!*"

"Well, I don't know what else to do!"

"They've been grumbling, haven't they?"

"Who?"

"Your friends."

"Well . . . a little. Eric and I had to make up some feeble story about a—"

"Then tell them the truth."

She flinched slightly. "What?"

"Tell them the truth. And I'll back you up. I promise. I'll—"

"I would appreciate it if someone would tell me the truth as well," Aunt Caroline said.

Sabrina gasped and spun around to see Aunt Caroline standing at the opening of the hallway in her robe and slippers. All she could do was stare silently at her aunt for what seemed an eternity.

"If you'll excuse us," Aunt Caroline said to Jeremy, "I'd like to speak with Sabrina alone for a moment." She turned and left the hallway.

Sabrina glanced at Jeremy, her mouth hanging open. She had no choice but to follow Aunt Caroline . . . and she did. She rounded the corner and found her aunt several yards away, sitting on the third step up on the staircase.

Aunt Caroline beckoned her with a pudgy-fingered hand.

Sabrina approached her haltingly, and finally sat beside her on the stair.

"Tell me the truth," Aunt Caroline said very quietly but firmly, looking directly into Sabrina's eyes with a stern expression. "What is Viktor up to?"

"How much did you hear?" Sabrina asked, her eyes widening as she leaned away from Aunt Caroline.

"That doesn't matter. What matters is that I have known Viktor ever since your mother married your father, which means I've known Viktor since before you were born. I've said nothing to anyone about him, because I'm in no position to judge anybody, that's not my place. But it has always been my feeling that there is something . . . well, uh . . ." She cleared her throat, bowed her head for a moment and touched a knuckle to her lips. "I've always felt that something is very, very wrong with Viktor," she said, lifting her head. "Something that has always nagged me to the very marrow of my bones. In fact, if you'd like to know the truth, Viktor has always—" She stopped and her eyebrows shot up suddenly. "You'll have to excuse my French, Sabrina, but Viktor has always scared the . . . the hell out of me." She pressed her lips together hard suddenly, as if she had swallowed an olive pit. "So, now . . . I expect you to tell me exactly what's going on, Sabrina. After all, I *am* your legal guardian. . . ."

About twenty minutes later, Sabrina led Aunt Caroline into the library, where everyone was still hard at work. She left the door open behind them.

"Okay, take a little break, everybody," Sabrina called.

They all stopped what they were doing and turned to her slowly.

"C'mon, chill out," Sabrina said, smiling. "Everybody, I'd like you to meet my Aunt Caroline. She is officially my legal guardian and she's going to be living here now."

Everyone smiled and greeted her . . . except for Eric. He looked at Sabrina with a frown. She gave him a wink.

"Well," Cheri said, "would you like us to keep this up, or what?"

"Not just yet. I want you to meet my dog." Sabrina whistled and snapped her fingers.

Through the open door loped a large dog. It was very furry and wolflike, the color of smoke from a chimney with piercing orange-colored eyes.

"This is my dog Jeremy," Sabrina said.

"*What*?" Eric blurted.

Everyone turned to him and he slapped a hand over his mouth, his eyes darting back and forth between the dog and the others.

Sabrina smiled as she said, "Well, Aunt Caroline's going to give us a hand, so I guess we can all get back to work and—"

"Wait a second," Chanelle said, perching a hand on her hip. "I hate to be a party pooper, but I'm getting pretty tired of this."

"I have to agree," Rob said. "This whole thing is awfully strange, Sabrina. It doesn't make much sense."

"Me, too," Cheri said, raising a hand as if she were in class. "I mean, we're looking for a book that's hidden somewhere in the *walls*? You know how many walls you've got in this house, Sabrina?"

Sabrina's smile disappeared as she nodded slowly and joined her hands before her. The dog sat on its haunches at her side, looking still and obedient. Aunt Caroline stood a couple steps behind her, looking patient.

"I thought you'd say that eventually," she said. "I just didn't think it would be this soon. It doesn't matter, I guess, because either way, I'd have to tell you the truth sooner or later. So, it might as well be sooner. Um . . . what if I were to tell you that the book we're looking for is sort of the, um, bible of black magic?"

No one moved. They stood like statues, staring at her with blank, unblinking eyes. Even Eric.

"And what if I told you that the reason we have to find it is that I have this uncle . . . well, he's *sort* of an uncle . . . who's a vampire because he was cursed by the witch who used to own that book . . . and that he plans to use that same curse on me to turn me into a vampire on my birthday. What would you think if I told you all that?"

Janna was the first to laugh, a long, high, musical laugh. She was immediately followed by Steve. In a moment, they were all laughing . . . all but Eric, who continued to stare at Sabrina as if he'd been hit in the back of the head with a shovel.

Sabrina looked down at the dog and said softly, "Jeremy."

The dog gave a gentle bark as it stood and went to the center of the large room. Standing there, mouth closed, the dog passed its bright orange eyes over the group . . . all except Eric. Then its legs collapsed and it crumpled to the floor.

Every one of them gasped as they stared at the apparently crippled animal. It began to convulse and it raised its face toward the ceiling as its wet-nosed snout began to shrink. The dog's pink tongue stuck out of the yawning, fanged mouth, quivering gelatinously as the entire body began to bulge.

The rest happened so suddenly that there was barely the time for the gasps that followed as a tall human figure rose from the shuddering mass of fur . . . and Jeremy stood in the center of the room, smiling at everyone.

Aunt Caroline stood behind Sabrina with both hands pressed firmly over her mouth.

The others stared at Jeremy with gaping mouths. Cheri whispered an obscenity; Janna clutched Rob's arm; Chanelle reached out to grab Steve's shoulder, but he had collapsed to the floor, conscious but weak-kneed.

"I think you'll all agree," Sabrina said, "that my story doesn't sound so funny now . . . right?"

They nodded, almost in sync.

"Okay, then," Sabrina said. "Maybe you'll listen if I tell you the *whole* story?"

She got no arguments from anyone, including Aunt Caroline and Eric.

Jeremy stood in the middle of the room and continued to smile, apparently quite amused. . . .

TWENTY-FOUR

The Destruction Goes On . . . and On

After witnessing Jeremy's transformation, none of them doubted anything Sabrina had to say, and she told them everything. Aunt Caroline, who wasn't used to having servants or household help of any kind, went out and made them a pot of coffee, then brought it in on a large tray with cups and served each of them. After a long silence during which they sipped their coffee and looked at one another as if each of them had just been slapped, they went back to work. But now they approached the dismantling of the library with an enthusiasm they had not shown before.

As the night grew later, they went to the phone, one by one, to call home and say they would be late.

Eventually, they tired out, and it got too late for them to stay any longer. After all, they had to go back to work the next day. But they all promised to come back after work tomorrow and continue what they'd started.

They were very serious as they left—they even looked a bit afraid—and each of them hugged Sabrina on the way out.

Once they were gone, Sabrina turned to face Eric, Jeremy, and a very tired-looking Aunt Caroline.

"Well, I don't know about you guys," she said, "but I'm exhausted."

"Me, too," Eric agreed.

With a sigh, Aunt Caroline said, "I think I could pass out on the spot."

Jeremy said with a smile, "I, however, am up for the night. As usual. I'll keep looking in the library, if you want."

Sabrina nodded, then turned to Eric. "You want me to drive you home?"

"Absolutely not. Your birthday's about half an hour away and you'd have to drive home alone."

"He's right," Jeremy said. "As of midnight tonight, it's open season on you."

"I should go home tonight, though," Eric said. "If you don't mind, I'll take your car."

"No problem."

Eric looked at Jeremy and Aunt Caroline. "You'll keep an eye on her?"

They promised they would.

Sabrina walked him out to the car.

It was a bone-chilling night. A light drizzle fell through the souplike mist that oozed over the top of the hill.

Beside the car, Sabrina embraced Eric and held him close.

"I'm so scared," she whispered. "I remember when I used to look forward to my birthday, but this time . . ."

"Don't worry," Eric whispered into her ear. "Everything's gonna be—"

His words stuck in his throat as the sound of flapping wings passed over them in the mist. They both stiffened and slowly looked upward, but they could see nothing.

The sound faded slowly . . . *very* slowly.

"It-it was probably juh-just an owl, or something," Sabrina whispered tremulously.

"Yeah," Eric muttered, "an owl, or . . . something." Suddenly, with an arm around her shoulders, he led her away from the car and back up the front steps to the door. "Okay, that's it. I know you're scared, but so am I. I'm so scared I'm about to wet myself. And I won't sleep tonight unless I know for *sure* that you're okay. So I'll stay another night."

"You don't have to—"

"Yes I do. I'll call my parents. They'll understand. They're very sympathetic toward your situation. They'll think I'm a great guy for helping out my friend. They won't know that I'm shaking like a little kid in the dark."

At the top of the steps, Sabrina spun around in front of him, stopping him in his tracks, took his face between her hands and gave him a long kiss. When she pulled away, she didn't pull away very far.

"You're pretty great, you know that?" she whispered.

A smile grew slowly on his lips. "So are you. You don't think I'd go through this for a girl who was just mediocre, do you?"

She laughed quietly as they went back inside. . . .

* * *

The next day was a rainy one. The rain fell in great, angry sheets, cutting through the misty air at an angle.

Eric had spent the night in the empty bedroom next to Sabrina's with his door open so he could hear her should she call for him. But the night had passed uneventfully, and after breakfast, Sabrina and Eric returned to the library and went back to work.

By late afternoon, the library looked as if someone had driven a semi through it . . .

. . . and they had found nothing.

The two of them sat Indian style in the middle of the floor, their faces, hair, hands, and clothes powdered with plaster dust.

"This seems so impossible," Sabrina said. "I mean, look how long it took us to tear up *this* room. Can you imagine how long it'll take us to go through the entire house?"

Eric said nothing; there was nothing he *could* say.

After a long silence, Sabrina frowned and asked, "What do you think my parents meant in that letter?"

"Meant by what?"

"Well, it said something about them—my parents—being closest to the treasure. I think it said, 'remember that closest to that treasure are your parents'."

Eric thought about it. "Where did they spend most of their time?"

She shrugged. "Dad spent a lot of time in here. He spent even more time next door in his study."

"Maybe we should try that room next."

Sabrina only sighed, closing her eyes wearily.

Eric leaned over and gave her a gentle kiss. "Happy birthday, by the way," he said with a smile.

She tried to smile back, but failed. "Yeah. Happy."

Shortly after dinner, the others arrived, and together, they began to take the study apart just as they had the library the night before. . . .

TWENTY-FIVE

Distress Call

Two hours after Jeremy had joined them, Eric called him aside and the two of them crossed the mostly demolished study to step out into the hallway.

"I don't know about you," Eric whispered, "but I'm a little worried. I mean, this *is* Sabrina's birthday, and there's not much left of it by now. Viktor hasn't even shown himself."

"I know, that worries me, too. I'd be more comfortable if I knew what the hell he was up to."

"It seems like we should be *doing* something."

"We are," Jeremy said with a fanged smile. "We're tearing up the house. That's about all we *can* do at the moment." He put a hand on Eric's shoulder and led him back into the study. . . .

They decided to take a break and have some coffee in the dining room, worn out after nearly four hours of tearing apart the study. Eric went to the cordless phone in the front of the house to call his parents. They hadn't seen him in days, and he wanted to make sure they weren't worried or anxious. They were very understanding, but even with the best of parents, sometimes compassion went only so far.

"Hi, Mom, it's me," he said when she answered. He was unable to hide the weariness in his voice.

"Oh, honey, you sound so tired."

"No, I'm okay. We've just been helping Sabrina to look for, um . . . well, something in the house that used to belong to her parents. We've been—"

"That's all right, Eric, you don't have to explain. I think what you've been doing is wonderful, and so does your dad. It's nice to see old friends sticking together like that. Mr. Van Fleet says you've been a big help to Sabrina and we think—"

"Mr. *who?*" Eric blurted.

"Mr. Van Fleet, Sabrina's uncle. He dropped by to thank us for letting you spend so much time with Sabrina since her parents, uh . . . well, you know."

"He's *there?* In the *house?*"

"Yes. We're having coffee. He's a very nice man." She lowered her voice a bit, and Eric could hear her smile in her voice. "And so cultured and good-looking, too. I thought it was nice of him to come by for—"

Eric didn't hear the rest of her sentence. He was walking frantically in a small circle, his hand clutching the phone so tightly that his knuckles were the color of sour milk. His mind had shut down for a moment and his palms were sweating.

"I should get off the phone, honey," she said. "It's not polite to talk on the phone while company is—"

"No, *no*, Mom, don't hang up! Um, just a second, I-I-I've gotta, um . . . just hang on a second."

He lowered the receiver with a hand over the mouthpiece, trying to think.

Viktor was finally making his move. Eric didn't know what that move was yet, but Viktor had had the gall to involve Eric's family.

"Can I talk to him for a second?" Eric asked.

"Well, yes, but . . . are you all right, Eric?"

"I'm fine, really, I just want to talk to Viktor."

She sounded uncertain. "Okay, but . . . you're sure you're—"

"Please put him on the phone, Mom," Eric said, his voice a little higher than usual as it squeezed through his constricting throat.

After a long moment, Viktor's deep voice came over the phone: "Hello, Eric, my boy."

"Get away from my family, damn you!" Eric barked.

Viktor released a long, cold chuckle that sounded like pebbles rattling around inside the cordless receiver. "I am afraid that is out of the question. I have been enjoying myself far too much. Your mother and father have been very hospitable. And your little brother? Oh, he is a fine young man."

"What the hell are you doing?" Eric's voice was hoarse now, breaking under the stress that was making his heart pound furiously.

"My, my, Eric. That is harsh language for a boy who comes from such a fine, pleasant family."

"I *said*, what the—"

"I want you to pay attention to me. You ignored me the last time I talked to you. It would be very unwise to do so this time."

"Okay, okay, look, just . . . I just want to know what you want." His knees were shaking and he leaned his shoulder against a wall as he rubbed his eyes with an unsteady hand.

"I want you and my lovely niece to join us for coffee. Right now."

Eric tried to catch his breath for a moment. "Listen, I'll come. Really, I'll be right over. You can do whatever you want to me as long as you let my family go. But . . . I-I won't bring Sabrina."

"Then you will arrive home to find yourself a brotherless orphan."

Suddenly, Eric's stomach turned over and he felt sick.

"As I said, Eric, it would be foolish for you to take this lightly. I want a trade. You have something I need . . . and I have something you need. I think that is quite simple. I will see you soon, Eric. With Sabrina. And *no one else*."

There was a soft click and the connection was severed.

Eric dropped the receiver onto its table in the phone nook and headed for the dining room, trying to catch his breath. He staggered drunkenly, clumsily slamming his shoulder into a doorjamb, bumping a chair here, a table there.

He didn't know what to do. Viktor had him up against a wall. Eric was being forced to choose between the people he cared for the most in the world . . . and it seemed there was no way out.

Once he'd gotten Sabrina and Jeremy out of the dining room and away from the others, they returned to the torn-up study. Although she hadn't been invited, Aunt Caroline followed them with a stern look in her eyes and listened as Eric told them what had just happened and everything Viktor had said. Sabrina put an arm around him as he talked. Eric was so visibly upset, she was afraid he might collapse.

Jeremy, however, kept his calm as he listened intently, and when Eric was finished, he said, "Okay, I'll come with you."

"No, you *can't*!" Eric insisted. "Viktor said he just wanted the two of us and no one else."

"Oh, dear God," Aunt Caroline whispered as she closed her eyes for a moment.

"I won't go in the car," Jeremy said. "I'll follow you by air. And I won't go in with you right away, either. But I can't let you face him alone. You can't believe a word he says. Once you arrive, he might decide to kill you and your whole family, then take Sabrina. No, you're *not* going without me. Just leave the front door open behind you when you go in. I'll be there watching and listening. I'm not going to let anything happen to your family *or* Sabrina . . . if I can help it."

"I'll drive," Sabrina told Eric. "You're too upset."

"*I'm* upset?" Eric said. "*You're* the one he wants!"

"Don't worry about me," she said, clutching his elbow as she led him out of the study. "Let's get going."

Jeremy followed them as they left the house. . . .

*　*　*

Aunt Caroline rushed back to the dining room, where everyone was gathered around the table drinking coffee and eating muffins.

"Listen, everyone," she said. "I need your help. So does Sabrina. Does anyone here know where Eric lives?"

They all said "yes" simultaneously.

"Good. I'll need someone to drive me over there. But first, let's get back into the study. I need you boys to break the legs off that credenza. And you"—she pointed to Cheri —"get me a hammer and a couple nails."

None of them knew what was going on, but they headed for the study instantly as Aunt Caroline shouted, *"And let's hurry!"*

TWENTY-SIX

Viktor's Trade

I t was raining so furiously that the windshield wipers could scarcely keep the glass clear on Sabrina's car. She drove as quickly as she could, considering the weather, and it wasn't long before she came to a stop at the curb in front of Eric's house.

"Listen to me," Eric said. He'd calmed down somewhat, but his voice was still hoarse. "I'll go in first. You stay outside the door until I call for you."

"But Viktor wants me, not—"

"This is nonnegotiable! Now, let's go."

As they got out of the car, they both looked up into the rain and all around them to see if they could spot Jeremy, but he was nowhere in sight. . . .

Eric stepped into the house, leaving the front door half open behind him, and found the living room dark except for the flickering glow of the blaring television. His parents and Nick were seated on the sofa . . .

. . . but their heads were craned back, their mouths hung open and their bodies were completely motionless.

"Oh, God!" Eric exclaimed as he started toward them, arms outreached as if to embrace them. He felt dizzy all of a sudden, because he was certain they were dead.

"They are perfectly fine."

Eric stumbled to a halt and spun toward the deep voice.

Viktor was in the recliner, his elbows on the arm-rests, his fingers steepled beneath his chin, eyes staring at the television screen. He was wearing his Inverness coat, but looked as relaxed as a man kicking back in his bathrobe.

"They are in a state of unconsciousness," he went on. "And they will come out of it. They will be perfectly healthy and will not remember a thing. It will simply be another evening at home. But that will only happen if you do as you are told."

Eric looked back and forth between his family and Viktor, then he stepped toward the smiling man, angered by the sight of him in Dad's recliner. With fists clenched at his sides, Eric took in a breath to speak, but no words came to him.

"I never watch television," Viktor said casually. "I thought it was a silly invention to begin with, of course . . . but I never realized it was very, very *bad*. Ah, well." He sighed, getting to his feet. "That is neither here nor there. Where is Sabrina?"

"She's here," Eric said. "But first, I want to know what you're going to . . . to do with her."

"That, my boy, is none of your concern. I told you before, you are not a part of this family. The business of the Van Fleet family is not yours." He took two broad steps and stood a couple inches from Eric, towering over him. "Now. Where is my niece?"

"She's . . . not your niece," Eric croaked through clenched teeth.

Viktor's upper lip twitched until it pulled back over his fangs, which reflected the multicolored glow of the television in tiny glimmers. He suddenly shot out his right arm and clutched Eric's throat with his big hand.

"Listen, boy," he growled, his voice sounding like that of a wolf that had suddenly gained the power of speech. "You have reached the limit of my patience and I am going to—"

"I'm right here, Uncle Viktor," Sabrina said.

Viktor released Eric immediately and looked at her. Eric spun around to look at her as well, massaging his throat absently. She stood just inside the front door.

"I'm here," she said, "so you can leave Eric alone now. He did what you told him to do."

Viktor smiled, his eyes locked on Sabrina. Suddenly, he behaved as if Eric wasn't there at all.

"Sabrina," he whispered. "How nice of you to come."

Moving toward Sabrina very slowly, Viktor began to sing in a quiet voice, "Happy birthday . . . to you . . ."

Eric watched in horror as the distance between Viktor and Sabrina began to close.

". . . happy birthday . . . to you . . ."

Eric didn't know what to do! Where was Jeremy? Eric knew he couldn't stand up to Viktor himself! He

glanced at his family, lined up like corpses on the sofa
. . . then at Sabrina, who now had a strange look in her
eyes . . . the same look she'd had when they'd faced
Viktor in the basement. . . .

". . . happy birthday . . . dear Sabrina . . ."

Anger and fear burned in Eric's gut like acid. He
threw caution to the wind and made his next move
without even giving it a thought. He dove forward,
jumped on Viktor's back and began pounding his fists
into Viktor's face from behind.

Viktor did not even miss a step. With a single flick of
his shoulder, he sent Eric flying backward onto the recliner. Eric rolled over one of the armrests and flopped
to the floor, feeling as if he'd just been hit in the chest
with a cannonball.

". . . happy birthday . . . to . . . yooouuu."

Viktor stood before her, very close, and placed his
right hand on top of her head, splaying his long fingers
out over her skull.

He began to speak, once again, in that gibbering,
foreign tongue. What came out of his mouth sounded
more like the babblings of an insane asylum inmate
rather than words.

Sabrina's head tilted backward and her eyes closed,
almost reverently, as if she were being baptized. Her
mouth yawned open as her jaw fell slack.

"No," Eric said . . . but his voice was nothing more
than a whimper. He tried to get up, but his body was as
unsteady as a pile of unsolidified Jell-O.

Where is Jeremy? Eric thought. *Where the hell is—*

Suddenly, there was a sound in the rainy darkness

outside the front door. It was the low growl of an animal, vicious and threatening.

Eric fought to lift his head, and when he succeeded, he could see the orange eyes glimmering just outside the door.

Viktor's gibbering chant stopped and he looked beyond Sabrina to the open door. He chuckled as he gently pushed Sabrina—stiff-backed, eyes now half closed, with a stunned look on her openmouthed face—aside and took a step forward.

Suddenly, the darkness framed by the doorway seemed to explode with movement as an enormous wolf shot into the house toward Viktor, *onto* Viktor, who stumbled backward as he wrapped his arms around the creature defensively and let out a horrible growl of his own.

The two of them moved around the living room in a jerky dance of death, snarling, growling . . . fangs flashed in the darkness . . . Viktor's arms rose and fell, one after the other as the wolf snapped at his face again and again, until . . .

. . . Viktor got the upper hand in the blink of an eye and he slammed the wolf's back against a wall, shattering the glass of a framed collage of family photos. The collage dropped to the floor and Viktor sprayed the wolf's suddenly desperate face with saliva as he spoke, closing his hand on the wolf's throat, squeezing his thumb and fingers tightly.

"You have no power over me, Jeremy!" he roared. *"You are not even an equal! I thought you knew that by now!"* The wolf was making sputtering, choking sounds, its

pink tongue lolling from one side of its snout. "You are nothing more than a servant in waiting, and I will use you when I see fit! Until then, stay out of my way, Jeremy. I had the power to make you what you are . . . I also have the power to snuff you out like a candle flame."

The wolf's eyes began to close.

Viktor threw the animal aside and it fell in a motionless heap to the floor. In seconds, the body began to bulge and change and stretch and . . .

. . . Jeremy lay sprawled on the floor, unconscious.

Eric's head fell back in defeat.

Viktor returned to Sabrina and put his hand back on her head. He continued his litany in a low, rumbling voice.

Eric struggled to move. He managed to prop himself up on an elbow . . . then got to his hands and knees. He began to crawl slowly, weakly, toward Viktor.

What are you going to do when you get there, you idiot? he thought.

He didn't know. But he knew he was the only one who might be able to help Sabrina now that Jeremy was out of commission. Of course, Eric knew full well that his chances of accomplishing anything were, without the help of a miracle, slim.

The chanting continued . . . Sabrina began to make tiny panting sounds that gurgled in her throat . . . Eric continued to crawl forward with every muscle in his body feeling like melted butter . . . until he finally collapsed.

He realized then that he'd moved less than a couple feet. There was nothing he could do.

Viktor was going to have his way and Eric was going to lose Sabrina . . . and maybe even his family. . . .

TWENTY-SEVEN

A Surprise
Guest

Jeremy felt himself slipping, felt his consciousness leaving him as he lay on the living room floor . . . when the room was suddenly filled with the sound of a loud, commanding, female voice.

"Get away from her!"

Eric struggled to lift his head . . . and he could not believe what he saw.

Aunt Caroline stood in the doorway, both hands wrapped firmly around a makeshift cross made out of two pieces of wood. There were others behind her, shapes moving in the darkness, but Eric couldn't make them out.

Holding the cross before her, elbows locked, Aunt Caroline said once again, *"Get away from her!"*

The next sound that came from Viktor sounded like the roar of a lion. He jerked his hand from Sabrina's head and she collapsed like a deflated balloon. Viktor staggered backward, raising a protective arm before his face.

But he didn't move backward as quickly as Aunt Caroline moved forward.

She lifted her arms and brought the large cross down on Viktor hard, as if she were squashing an enormous bug.

Then the sound coming from Viktor's throat became more human: it was a high, strangled scream.

The scream began to echo, as if it were traveling through a long tunnel, and Viktor began to *glow*! It lasted only a moment, this bluish-orange glow that came over his body . . .

. . . then he burst into a quiet explosion of bluish-orange flames which rose from the floor in a fiery ball that lit up the dark room.

The ball of fire shot out of the open door like a bullet.

There were shocked, fearful exclamations outside the door.

Then silence.

It was at that moment that Eric's consciousness left him and the room's darkness got even deeper. . . .

When he awoke, he was lying on the sofa. His mother's smiling face was hovering over him, and beside her was Sabrina. He sat up with a jerk, eyes wide, and looked around to see his dad, Nick, Chanelle, Steve, Janna, Rob, Cheri, Aunt Caroline, and Jeremy. The living room was crowded. He looked at them with a shocked expression and was about to speak when he saw Jeremy lift a finger to his lips, silently telling Eric to say nothing about *anything*.

"You passed out, honey," Mom said. "Are you okay?"

"Uh . . . yeah. Yeah, I'm fine."

"He's just been paying too much attention to me and too little to himself," Sabrina said with a smile.

"But he's been such a support to all of us," Aunt Caroline said. "I don't know what Sabrina would have done without him."

Eric tried to stand.

"Maybe you should just lie down," Dad said.

"No, really, I'm okay, I'm, uh . . . just a little tired, I guess."

Mom said, "Caroline told us how hard you've all been working to find that heirloom in the house."

Eric blinked. "The, uh, heirloom. Yeah."

She leaned forward and whispered to him, as if it was just between the two of them, "I think it's great you've been helping Sabrina out. She needs it. If you want to go back over there, that's fine, we don't mind. But only if you're well enough. I want you to take care of yourself."

Eric nodded and Mom backed away as Eric got to his feet.

As Sabrina gave him a hug she whispered very softly in his ear, "No, you didn't dream it all. This isn't *The Wizard of Oz*. Everything's fine, just go along with all this, okay?"

He nodded again.

"Who would like some coffee?" Mom asked. "I completely forgot I've got a pot of it in the kitchen."

Everyone smiled and said yes. . . .

Epilogue

They sat around the table in Sabrina's dining room later that night. Everyone chatted, making nervous small talk, as if they were all too exhausted to have a real conversation. They were.

Sabrina sat at the head of the table, saying nothing. She wore a contented smile as she looked from one of them to another.

How did I get so lucky? she wondered. *How many other people have this many friends who would be so willing to help out in a situation this . . . this insane?*

Then she looked at Eric and a feeling of warmth grew inside her. Suddenly, she reached over and took his hand, squeezing it tightly.

The chatter ceased when Jeremy spoke in a serious voice.

"I want to make sure everybody understands something," he said. "What happened tonight was . . . well, it was pretty amazing. I don't know what we would've done without Aunt Caroline. But Viktor's still out there somewhere. Sabrina is now officially the head of this house, not to mention the owner, so Viktor can't come in here unless"—he turned to Sabrina—"unless you invite him."

"It'll be a cold day in hell before *that* happens!" Sabrina said.

"I know. But that doesn't mean he's through. We don't know what other tricks he's got up his sleeve. He still wants the *Black Grimoire* . . . and he still wants you, Sabrina. The only way we can keep him from getting what he wants is to find that book first . . . and use it against him."

There was a long silence around the table.

"Well, then," Sabrina said. "I guess we should get back to work. . . ."

To be continued in:

DEADLY RELATIONS

About the Author

JOSEPH LOCKE is a former English teacher and the author of *Kill the Teacher's Pet*, *Petrified*, *Kiss of Death*, *Game Over*, *Vengeance*, and *1-900-Killer*. He, his wife, Logan, and their dog, Tucker, divide their time between Eureka, California—where they spend their spare time combing beaches and exploring tide pools—and the Napa Valley. He is currently working on his next novel.

Read at your own risk.
You may be
SCARED TO DEATH
Who is Bobby Wimmer stalking and why?